ROCK 'N ROLL

"Hit the deck," Rockson shouted. He and his Freefighters all dove down as the razor-brimmed hats of the fanatic protectors sailed over their heads. Archer twisted around and managed to get one of his steel explosive arrows notched and in the air. He skewered a row of fanatic killers headed his way.

Rockson decimated a flock of protectors with a series of shots from his shotpistol. They fell, peppered with the "X" patterned explosions of his special smg bullets. Chen downed another three with a single shuriken explosive star dart. And, as Detroit lobbed grenades to keep the other screaming enemies back, the Doomsday Warrior and his men rushed forward for the final battle.

THE SURVIVALIST SERIES
by Jerry Ahern

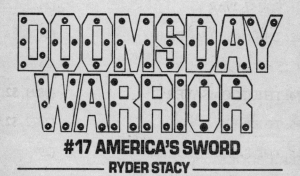

#17 AMERICA'S SWORD

RYDER STACY

ZEBRA BOOKS
KENSINGTON PUBLISHING CORP.

ZEBRA BOOKS

are published by

Kensington Publishing Corp.
475 Park Avenue South
New York, NY 10016

First printing: January, 1990

Printed in the United States of America

Chapter One

One second everything was normal, the next it was a living hell. Ted Rockson, a/k/a the Doomsday Warrior, was lying in his bed, down in one of Century City's lower levels, in that pleasant state between sleeping and waking. One eye was slightly open, the other closed, still trying to cling to the soft darkness of the dream he had just been swimming in. Then the whole world was most rudely and noisily pulled into stark reality. There was a thundering roar that bolted both eyes open in a flash, and then the lights went out.

Rockson was looking up at a cloud of dust that was streaming down from the low ceiling above. Instantly a huge crack appeared almost right above his bed in his 12 x 15 sleeping quarters. Then as he watched with horror in the dim red light of the room's emergency lighting system, he saw the crack widen and spiderweb out in all directions. Within a second or two the entire ceiling was bending down as if reaching below for the occupant of the room, to crush him into pulp.

"Earthquake," Rockson's mouth muttered without

his even quite realizing he had spoken the words. His brain was a bit slower than his lips, but it instantly realized in a flash what the word "earthquake" meant. It meant he would be crushed to death in milliseconds if he didn't move his butt faster than a hawk dropping for a kill. Even as he started to rise up, his mind feverishly wondering just where to hide, the thunder grew ever-louder, vibrating up his skull, hurting his ears as if he were inside a storm cloud. The whole room began shaking and moving around so that he hardly knew where he was. Out of his peripheral vision Rockson could see the radio bouncing off the table, and the clock dancing around like it was in a tango contest. Then a picture of an ancient whaling ship, something that he had dug up in his travels, flew right off the wall like it was trying to get back to the sea.

The cracked ceiling above him made a most threatening sound, not dissimilar to a few hand grenades going off, and Rock knew he was out of time. Although his brain didn't seem to know just how the hell to deal with all this, his mutant body acted with its own agenda. For even as the bed shook more wildly, Rock rolled over the side of it and underneath, unconsciously knowing that the thing had a steel frame and might offer protection. Even as he hit the floor and pulled himself under, he knew that it was a chance in a million—but it was all he had. The room was just a small rectangle with nowhere to run, nowhere to hide.

Rock made his move with not a moment to spare. The instant he slid under the bed, the entire ceiling came smashing down like he was at ground zero of a nuke bomb test. The room shook wildly. Everything

6

was just darkness, crunching sound, and broken concrete flying all over the place like a hurricane of cement—from particles as small as marbles to as big as huge slabs. Two of the slabs came falling at each end of the bed, crushing it down on top of him. Rock knew he would die at any second and took a final sharp intake of breath, as if he didn't want to go into the next world without a little oxygen still in his lungs.

As he lay there, in an awkward sideways position, his hip pressed hard against the floor which he could also feel shaking and cracking around him, the vibrations continued. They seemed to get stronger so that his very bones were being batted around inside of his flesh. Somehow through the dust he saw the entire wall that separated his sleeping chamber from the outer corridor crack all over like a huge gray egg. Then just as it collapsed, more of the ceiling came down and all he could see was jagged chunks of what had once been his room, slamming into the floor just inches from his face.

He pulled back hard, or tried to, realizing even in the madness and confusion of the destruction, that at least thus far the bed frame had provided a sort of shelter for him. He tried to pull deeper into the darkness beneath, like a child delving deeper under his covers, hoping that that would somehow protect him from the nightmares of life, real and imagined. He realized he was stuck, wedged in from all sides by the bed and pieces of concrete ceiling that had fallen on and around it. Rockson shut his eyes to protect them from the dust.

Then just as suddenly as it had started, the quake, or whatever the hell it was, stopped. There were a few more shudders, then a series of undulations, very mild

7

almost as if the walls of Century City were alive. Then it was still. And the screams rose up everywhere out in the halls and the other sleeping quarters. It was a terrible sound, men and women trapped in the sheer animal agony of excruciating pain.

But Rockson had his own problems to worry about. Trapped as tightly as a beaver in a steel cage, he tried to move and couldn't. Everything, every part of him felt wedged down beneath the collapsed bed. It had saved him from being totally crushed, but he could feel it pushing down all over him. Everything hurt, but somehow, just because he could feel the different parts of his body, if not move them, he figured he hadn't any major damage. So far.

Suddenly he began coughing, hacking away as the dust and concrete particles reached deep into his throat. It hurt, burning his lung tissue and his throat like flecks of fire. He hacked away for a good thirty seconds, bringing up all kinds of garbage from below, including, by the slick feel of it, some blood. He was completely coated with dust and junk. It was as if there was no air, just soot finely crushed with a few atoms of oxygen thrown in here and there just to taunt him. He felt himself start to cough again, and, using every bit of will power, somehow suppressed the urge.

Rock tried to open his eyes, which were just as much covered with the leftovers of the collapse. They burned terribly; he could feel them coated with dust from corner to corner. He blinked hard but that only seemed to sort of press everything harder against the skin. His hand had ended up wedged against the side of his cheek just inches from his face. By twisting and shimmying

8

slowly and carefully so as not to dislodge what might well be a precarious balancing act of debris above him, Rock managed to get his index finger near his lips. He spat, but not a hell of a lot happened.

He tried again and after a few hacking attempts, a gob of spit landed on his finger and began sliding over it.

Quickly Rock lifted the spit-coated finger to his eye and lightly rubbed it into the corners. It took several attempts and a lot of coughing up, but at last he had both eyes cleared enough to see. And Rockson realized that he might as well have saved his spit. There was nothing to see. Just gray dust that floated evenly in the air everywhere.

There was the slightest dim yellow glow coming from the corridor, but it wasn't much, a thousandth of a lumen; enough for a worm to see by. Now that everything had calmed down at least for a few seconds, he began realizing the total severity of his situation. He was trapped deep beneath the ground, in one of Century City's lower levels. God only knew how much of the city had collapsed, how many were alive. He could hear screams coming from outside his room.

Suddenly he couldn't breathe again. It was hard to tell if it was the dust that was everywhere or the contracting of his lungs as they sucked harder and harder for less and less air. And for one of the few times in his life Ted Rockson felt a deep terror sweep through him. A fear that a child feels when nightmares attack. A fear that can paralyze a man's heart and make his body clamp up like a vise, his muscles shake, his blood boil inside. He could feel himself losing it, losing his center.

Buried alive. A ghastly and hideous fate. And as the dust seemed to clog his lungs more by the second and fill his eyes and ears with gritty, clinging particles, Rock knew that that was exactly what was about to happen to him. He was going to be buried alive like a corpse beneath the cold concrete.

Chapter Two

Rockson lay in a sort of limbo zone between consciousness and unconsciousness. With the dust filling the air everywhere in a blanket of darkness, and hardly any air to move it all around, his prospects looked bleak. The Doomsday Warrior had never quite realized how much one's consciousness, one's very being, depended on sensory information coming in from the outside world. But here, trapped beneath God only knew how many tons of rubble, there was nothing coming in. The dust stopped all but the dimmest trickles of gray light from a few cracks in the far wall, probably one of the hall emergency lights that had somehow survived the catastrophe. And the screams.

Without the stimulation of the world, it was as if he hardly existed. An embryo of fear, trapped in a womb of destruction and paralysis. He tried to breathe as slowly as he could, since when he took large breaths, he would also draw in large amounts of the dust, clogging his mouth, throat, and lungs, making him feel like he was suffocating. But when he could cool himself out even a little, and take very slow, even breaths, it seemed as if he could actually get some of the precious oxygen into his lungs. It helped a little, just that feeling that he had the slightest amount of control over his environment, even if it was at the bottom of a collapsed mountain.

Rockson had no way of knowing if the whole damn mountain had given way and Century City was now crushed beneath it all. Or if the whole world—everything—was gone. He knew it wasn't a nuke sent by the Reds, or there would have been a lot more heat generated. No, it had to be an earthquake or some fault in the geological structure beneath the mountain—a fault which moved a little too abruptly. Though it wasn't technically *that* earthquake zone there in the middle of the Rocky Mountains, at least he had always thought so. But a thousand, ten thousand years between quakes meant nothing to the Grim Reaper. He did what the hell he wanted.

Rock tried to keep his mind occupied, thinking about the different parts of the city, trying to visualize just what was out there now. Sometimes his telepathic abilities actually enabled him to see beyond his immediate surroundings. But not now. He had to be in a super-relaxed meditative state and that just wasn't happening at the moment. He'd be rescued. He had to believe that. There were work crews out there right now, no doubt digging their way down to him and the others trapped. Yes, for sure. He tried to hear, slowing his breath as much as possible, listening for any sound of help, of emergency crews slamming their tools through the concrete maelstrom. But there was nothing coming, nothing that sounded human anyway. Just the beating of his heart, and the occasional shifting of large slabs which made a grinding, terrible sound like a giant's fingernails on a chalk board.

There was another sudden shifting of the debris above him and Rockson felt the steel frame of the bed make all kinds of threatening noises like it was thinking of snapping in half. He knew if that happened, his days were over. Crushed into pâté that only the ants would enjoy. But though the frame gave some and he could feel a little more pressure on his lower left leg and foot, it held. Thank God, Dr. Shecter's manufacturing design people had made the things in Century City strong, to last for decades. If he ever got out of this dusty mess, he'd sure as hell thank the science chief of the city and his tech boys. If there was a city any more.

He had to stop thinking about them all, as their faces flashed before his dust-coated eyes. It was too much. He could deal with his own demise. It was hard, but God gave and took back again like a nervous shopper in a K-Mart universe. There wasn't a hell of a lot he could do about that, other than send up a few prayers. But the others, the city itself, ending! It was too much to allow himself to think about. President Langford, Kim—they were both here too, since they'd been rescued from Pattonville a month before. They were here all right, but he had no idea what state they were in. Against his will, Kim's delicate face flashed over and over in his mind like a neon sign gone mad. Only her face was crushed in, with bones poking out and blood all over the damn place.

Rockson gritted his teeth and with sheer force of will made himself think of other things. For some reason his mind drifted back, back through the years which

13

flipped and spun through his mind like leaves on the wind. Back to memories that were easier to deal with, memories filled with beauty, light, and no dust.

He was a child, back in the valley where he had spent his childhood. It was a harsh but stunningly beautiful world, with slopes filled with wildflowers, running brooks and wildlife abundant, and fresh air. For a landscape a hundred years after nuke war, one would never have known that such terror had occurred, that just a hundred miles in any direction there were craters and vast, scarred areas of land. Places where hardly a thing grew but for stunted and thorned trees with bark as thick and hard as steel.

He had been a wild child. Almost more of an animal than a human child. But his father had known that the mutant boy, with his white streak of hair running down the center of his jet-black name of hair and his mismatched aqua and violet eyes, was not like other children. He was tougher, stronger, faster. He needed the wildness of the surrounding hills and woods. And so he had let the boy Ted Rockson run free almost from the moment he could walk.

Rockson drifted back, ever deeper into the past, the past which was so much more preferable than the hell state he was in now. He was six, and was climbing Telegraph Peak, about eight miles from his valley home. Why they called it that, he didn't know, as there were no telegraphs or even the poles that had once carried such information. He climbed a rough-barked fir, the tallest of the tall trees that blanketed the slope, and at the very top he could see his house, the thin trickle of smoke rising easily into the tawny sky. Above, an eagle flew serenely on the wind, about five

14

hundred feet up, searching with its crystal eyes for prey. It caught his eye and for a flash the boy felt something like a charge between them, a current of life, of understanding of what the other was. An understanding that they were of the same wave, the same life-electricity that fueled all things.

Then the great golden-winged bird was off on an updraft, sensing the movement of something a mile or two off. And for a flash Rockson could see through the great bird of prey's eyes. He was up there too, looking down. And for a moment he felt dizzy, almost overwhelmed by the new perceptions. He would fall, he would crash down onto the trees. Then the cross-species perception was gone, and he let his pounding heart slow down again. If this was part of the legacy of being a mutant child, then so be it. He felt suddenly blessed and understood with a kind of childlike wisdom that he had to learn to allow such perceptions, such out-of-body experiences, to grow. That he was not like the other boys. For better or worse, he was different.

The scene in his mind suddenly changed. He was with his father, down by one of the nearby streams. Marston's Creek it was called, though no one could recall just who Marston was. They were fishing, and it was a perfect day with chandelier-crystal blue sky, not a cloud up there. A slow breeze wafted through the trees that grew on each bank of the easy-flowing water, and father and son were lying back lazily on their elbows as they waited for something to bite. His father was telling him about this and that, about how to find the best spot where the fish congregated, about dealing with women. About every kind of thing that a father

15

passes onto his son. And Rock felt lucky, incredibly lucky. He knew that this was a special, special moment. And he let it all in, soaked it up inside, his soul smiling.

Suddenly, against his will, the scene shifted again. He was ten years old, and was back in the small but comfortable cabin that he shared with his father, mother, and sisters. They were all cutting string beans, a red species that seemed to thrive since the nuke war, as the other green species had virtually all died out. Moose and bean stew was on the agenda for dinner; young Rockson's mouth was already watering as the triple-horned moose meat was being fried up slowly to get the juices out before being thrown into the huge stew pot nearly big enough for a young lad to bathe in—a fact which Rock's mother sometimes threatened him with when he got in trouble.

Suddenly everything had changed in just seconds. There were sounds outside the cabin, and as his father rushed to the window, he yelled to the family to hide.

"Reds," his father had yelled out. Just that word, a single sound, but it still reverberated through all the years. There weren't a hell of a lot of places to hide, but they all tried to find someplace, under a bed, inside a chest, as his father grabbed the family pump shotgun and stood inside the door, waiting. And they hadn't had to wait long. A squad of DeathShirts, the dreaded KGB murderers who roamed the countryside, killing and mutilating survivors, came smashing in. His father fired and took out two of them. Then he was sliced to bits. From beneath the floorboards, the young Rockson watched, tears streaming down his face, knowing he couldn't make a sound. Watched as his mother and sisters were raped, and then cut up like creatures for the slaughterhouse.

The image burned itself into his heart and mind as the tears coated his mouth and neck. His human heart wanted to leap up and attack them; he knew there was nothing he could do. He didn't have a chance against the seven murderers who carried out their bloody crimes. So he watched and memorized their faces, his eyes peering up from the darkness, unseen by the invaders. When they were done, there was nothing left of what had been his family. All the dreams and idyllic talks with his father, the scents of stew, wiped out in a matter of minutes. And Rockson as well was changed in those dreadful bloody moments. He became harder inside. Something inside of him died, and something else, an iron determination to live, and to fight the oppressor, was born.

When the scum finally left, Rock waited several minutes and then crawled out of his hiding place. He couldn't bear to look at what had happened to those he loved. But somehow, using the analytical side of his mutant nature, he overcame his fear. He wrapped each of his family up in sheets and buried them. It took almost a full day to do. Then he equipped himself with a few meager supplies, and a large hunting knife that had belonged to his father, and set the cabin on fire. He walked off without looking back.

Rockson's eyes suddenly flew open. He was back in the dust and debris of Century City, and tears were welling up in his eyes, just as they had decades ago. Memories lived so long, it was as if it had all just happened the day before. If he lived to be a hundred he would remember it, a nightmare in bloody technicolor. It took seconds to readjust to the here and now, so intense had the past been. He listened and looked to see if help was on the way. But it was all the same, just dust floating everywhere.

Suddenly, he heard a sound, as if something was moving near him. For a moment his heart speeded up with hope, his eyes opened a little wider as they searched through the dimness. But he saw instead something that made his gut turn over. A rat. No, a whole stream of them. His mutant eyes, able to collect ten times as much light as the eyes of "normals," were able to see the furry black shapes in the semidarkness as they scuttled around in the jagged debris of what had been his room. Rockson knew there had always been rats in Century City, but they had remained hidden away behind walls, down in their own secret labyrinths and tunnels. The city had always been kept clean with traps and cats. Until the walls came tumbling down.

"Shit," the Doomsday Warrior muttered through clenched teeth, not able to stand the vision of the bastards eating away at him, while he couldn't do a thing to stop them. He tried to pull back deeper under the bed as if that would hide him, which he knew even as he did so was a ridiculous gesture, as the rats could see better than he could in this light. There were hissing sounds as several of the vermin about three yards off sensed his motion and they stopped, staring hard. Their reddish eyes glowed like embers in the dust-fog, and Rockson gulped hard. How long would it take them to realize that he was unable to fight back?

Near panic, he felt something beneath his hip. Something hard, pushing against the bone. For a second he thought it was a piece of shattered concrete, but then realized as he brought his mind down to the spot, that the cold metal was his shotpistol. Somehow it had tumbled from the table beside his bed down with him when the whole world went crashing. Using every bit of strength and will he had, Rockson somehow managed to move his hand and shift his hip just a few inches. It took almost a minute to get it out and gripped in his hands. He watched the rats slowly edge in closer, looking at his face like it was going to be the first thing on the plate of delicacies. Many yards off, he heard a scream and prayed that the huge tunnel rats hadn't just taken a bite out of one of C.C.'s other citizens.

"Fucking back off, you slime-buckets," Rock yelled as one suddenly came charging in. The scream startled it, and it stopped and hissed, its fur rising up. Rock gripped the shotpistol and pulled it out from beneath him, causing excruciating pain to ripple down his body as he had to press against jagged pieces of cement everywhere. He got the thing firmly in grasp and aimed it in front of him. His scream had startled them, but now that they saw there was nothing to back it up, a whole horde of the toothy creatures came down the slabs of shattered ceiling while lay everywhere.

Rock pointed the pistol straight ahead, not even caring whether the shot ricocheted back onto him. If he was going to go, let it be from his own pistol, rather than from a thousand gnawing teeth. He pulled the trigger and there was a roaring boom that deafened him. By the light of the blast he could see there were hundreds of the wretched creatures spread out all around the debris. And they went flying as the shot poured into them. Furry bodies flew every which way like bloody ragdolls, heading into orbits, splattering on the collapsed walls, ramming into each other. Their squeals were deafening, then all was silent but for a few muted squeaks of pain.

Rock felt with his fingers around the side of the pistol. Two more shots left. Damn, why hadn't he reloaded the fucking thing last night, when he could have? He knew there were shells in the room. A lot of good that would do him now. They could have been inches away, but it was like a million miles. He was lucky to have even gotten the pistol. Already the unharmed rats were closing in again, gnawing on the butchered bodies of their compatriots. But there were too many of them; they would want more to eat. They seemed to pour out of every crevice in the grayness. A bunch came toward him again.

He held the pistol hard in his hands, wondering whether he should use it on himself, rather than on them. Seeing them ripping at the dead didn't exactly make him want to wait around to share the experience himself. And as they came in closer for the huge meal that awaited, Rockson's mind reeled back and forth as his finger tightened on the trigger.

Chapter Three

Rockson fired—at the rats. He knew he could never take his own life. It wasn't part of his soul. He'd go out fighting, biting at the little bastards as they did the same to him. Not that he didn't have trepidations to say the least. The final shot blasted through the wall of squealing fur that was coming at him and sent a good fifty of the carnivores shooting off like bloody meteors through the dust-choked room, hurtling into the distance where he could hear them slam against the wall. And then there were more squeals of pain, and of hunger. But it hardly seemed to slow the advancing ranks down. They seemed to be losing their fear of the weapon, not that the meat-eaters had a whole lot of fear built into their natures.

One of them suddenly leaped at his face from out of the dimness and Rockson somehow managed to whip the front of the pistol up, catching the thing on the side of the head so that it whimpered and flew sideways. But there were more where he came from. An army more. Another jumped, then another. One of them got in on the side of his face and took a nice bite right out of his cheek. Rockson let out with an involuntary yelp and shook his head wildly trying to dislodge it, though he could only move inches from side to side.

Suddenly he thought he heard something. A voice, several voices. Then above the squealing all around the room, scraping. He was sure of it. Men. They were digging him out. God was good to him today. If he could hang on. . . .

"Don't fire at us," a voice that sounded like Detroit's screamed out. "Who's down there? We heard some shots. Is that you, Rock? Who's there?" The voice sounded frightened, not for its owner, but for the fact that Rock might in fact be in there smashed to pulp beneath the fallen ceiling. He heard debris being frantically pulled about twenty feet off, shovels clanking cement and stone.

"Yeah, baby, it's me," the Doomsday Warrior screamed back as the rats hesitated from all the commotion. "And you better hurry, 'cause I got me some rats in here who are eyeing my face like they haven't been fed since before the big war."

"It's Detroit, Chief," the voice screamed back with real joy in the words. "Okay, man, we're coming in," the voice shouted through the fog of dust which still hung everywhere. "Just don't fire. Hang in there. We're sending in a little company while we try to reach you." Rockson couldn't figure out just what the hell kind of company that might be, since he couldn't remember someone skinny as a pole who could fit in the crevices and little snaky tunnels that were all he could see around him.

The rats sensed the newly arrived guests almost

22

instantly. Even the little bastard with its teeth flared back ready for a quick bite at Rockson's face. And as Rock saw the first of them coming out of the dust mist his face brightened as if the sun were shining through. Cats—big suckers, too! Cats that the rescue squads must have pulled up from the sub-levels where they had patrolled against rats and mice for years. The rats around Rockson, even though they outnumbered the prowling felines by hundreds to one, didn't exactly fancy facing off with any of these extra large mutant creatures, which had been bred for decades for their size and fearlessness and for their claws the size of mountain cats' claws!

There was hissing and snarling everywhere in the half-darkness that was lit fractionally here and there by beams from the lanterns. Men were digging through the hell zone toward him. A huge tom that looked more like a small dog than a feline came tearing straight at Rockson's face.

"Nice kitty," he announced, hoping the thing didn't think he was an oversized rat. At the last instant the forty-pound ball of muscle and teeth and claws leaped right up so that its tail whipped over his nose. It grabbed the rat which had been again thinking of doing something nasty to Rockson's cheek and snapped its neck. There was a cracking sound like a chicken bone breaking, then more of the snapping noises all around him, as the cats tore mercilessly through the ranks of would-be Rockson-eaters. The rats ran in every direction. Just survival was on their little minds.

"Where the hell are you, pal?" Detroit screamed out as Rockson heard sounds just a few yards off now and saw the lanterns, lights mounted on the crews' hardhats, illuminating the area where Rockson was trapped.

"Here, baby, over here," Rockson said, his face lit up like a Hawaiian sun at having survived. He slammed with the side of the pistol against a chunk of chair-sized concrete at the end of his outstretched arm. Rock could see the huge piece of smashed concrete right in front of him being lifted.

A bearded giant swung it around, and his eyes lit up to see what he'd uncovered.

"ROOCCKSSOON!" the huge near-mute bellowed out, dropping the concrete block to the side so the whole floor seemed to shake. Rock was never so glad to see an ugly, hairy face.

"Hey, easy pal," Detroit said, coming up behind him. "You almost got me on that last load!"

Archer's face couldn't stop grinning as he reached down to help Rock.

"Careful!" Detroit chastised the giant, pulling Archer back by the shoulder. "We've got to move slow so that we don't dislodge any of this junk piled atop him. Damn, mister, you've got a moving truck worth of jagged debris up here. How this bed frame held up I'll never know. Don't move."

"I ain't going nowhere," Rock grunted back.

They carefully took the pieces off him. Even with the giant and the black man with one bionic arm, it was tough work. Still, within just minutes they had almost the whole bed uncovered, the debris thrown to the side. Then came the bed frame which Archer lifted by himself and threw several yards.

"You okay, man?" Detroit asked, leaning down on one knee and handing Rockson some water from a

24

canteen and a wet compress for his eyes. Rockson sat up and took them both thankfully, drinking a few deep slugs to clear his throat of the grime and slunk. Then he flushed his eyes out and wiped his face clean. And he felt vaguely like something that was starting to resemble a man again.

"What the hell happened?" he asked as he handed the supplies back to Detroit and started to rise. "Was it a—?"

"Quake, huge one. Seven point three on the Richter scale; epicentered only twenty, maybe thirty miles from here. All things considered—we were lucky the whole damned place wasn't 100 percent destroyed."

"Damn," Rockson fell back to the floor as his foot seemed to give out. Archer caught him in midflight.

"What's wrong, Rock?" Detroit asked, anxiously, as he reached out an arm to support his field-commander.

"My fucking foot, I think it's broken or something," Rock said angrily.

"There's an emergency med-unit about a hundred yards behind us in the junction. They can fix it."

"How bad is it?" Rock asked as he hobbled along with Detroit's arm supporting him on one side.

"It's pretty damn bad," Detroit replied, "But well, you'll see."

Rock looked around. Everything they passed was like his quarters—collapsed, covered in sheets of dust. Subbasement real estate that wasn't worth diddly-shit any more.

"It's not this bad everywhere," the black Freefighter went on. "The main science chambers and much of the hospital are okay. The archives and library are supposedly fixable. Beyond that, I don't know."

Rockson winced and asked, "How many dead?"

Detroit sounded like he didn't want to answer. "A lot," he whispered.

"The President, Kim, Rona . . ." Rockson suddenly blurted out, a look of open fear on his face.

"We're looking man," Detroit said. "Once we get you taken care of, we'll be out again. Here we are," he said, as the two half-stumbled into the makeshift emergency treatment center.

It looked bad, all right. Bodies were piled on one side of the large chamber where all the tunnel systems of that level met in the middle and ramps ran up and down to the other twenty levels of the subterranean "Free-fighting city." Many were not alive—crushed beyond recognition. Only the fact that all the citizenry were identifiable both from finger and DNA holographs as well as from dental charts would enable anyone to I.D. them later. Some were crushed to pulp, just pieces of hands and tongues sticking out of the bloody piles of human horror. But they would all be identified, every last poor bastard of them.

Rock could hardly stand the screams as they entered the chamber. M.D.'s and nurses were operating right on the cots in the chamber. IV tubes, penicillin shots, and oxygen were being given out at a frantic rate by whoever was hobbling around. Bones were broken everywhere, some men's limbs hanging at grotesque angles. It was a mess, that was damn sure.

They somehow found Rock a cot and a doctor came rushing over, seeing who it was. Rank did have its privileges.

"Gonna split, man," Detroit said as soon as he saw Rockson was in the right hands. "Don't have time to talk when there's so much—"

Rock waved him on, not even wanting to talk. Archer came grumbling on behind the black man as they headed out to search for more survivors.

"What's up, Rock?" the doctor asked, as he stopped just in front of the Doomsday Warrior.

"My left foot, Doc. Think I might have mashed it up good in the collapse."

"Well, let me take a look." The doctor began removing the boot and Rockson winced in pain. "I'll have to cut the boot off," the doc said, taking out a small laser-saw, one of Shecter's inventions. He sliced through the thick leather in an instant, not touching a hair on Rockson's calf or leg. He removed the boot and looked down at the foot, then turned it slightly a few inches in each direction as Rock yelped.

"Yeah, it's a break." He took out a hypo-pad and stabbed the ankle and foot with it a few times.

"Multishot," the doctor commented. "Has every antibiotic, vitamin, numbing and healing agent known to man. Should stop infection from setting in." He sprayed all the wounds over with a thin layer of plastic medicine which hardened to a rubberlike texture. Then he made a small cast, taking what looked like a construction caulking gun. He squeezed the trigger and a thick, goppy mess came out over Rock's foot. Before it hardened, the doc pulled Rock's foot into proper position.

"Instant cast," he said, looking down with a thin smile. Rock looked down at the doctor's handiwork. It had already hardened before his eyes. But though Rockson was happy enough to still have his foot, he could see the injury was going to slow him down.

"How long before I can get up on it?" Rock asked.

"Maybe give it twenty minutes and it'll reach max-strength. After that, you'll have to keep it on at least two weeks. Then just cut it off. I'll give you one of those laser-cutters; it will make it easy."

"Have you heard anything about the President? Kim? Rona?" Rockson asked, anxious again.

"Nothing yet! But Rockson, the quake's less than a few hours old. They're still finding survivors. Depends on where—"

"Yeah, relax," Rockson said with a sneer, though he knew the doctor meant well. "Thanks for the quick fix."

The Doomsday Warrior jumped down from the cot, once he saw that the foot cast had hardened enough to take his weight. He felt a numb throbbing, but at least he could move.

He hobbled through streams of wounded. It was like another nuclear bomb had gone off. And Rockson felt even his spirit sag somewhere deep inside. So much destruction after so many years of labor and love spent to build it all up. It had been a beautiful city, the pride of all of America's Freefighting hidden cities. And now . . . nothing but the broken, the dying and dead.

Chapter Four

That evening, around crude kerosine lanterns spread out on a huge square table, about fifty men sat with deeply pensive expressions on their faces. Men whose eyes all looked like they had just been given a glimpse of hell, and would just as soon not have seen it. Not when it was their own wives and children, their own homes that had been squashed to human paste and ripped, destroyed, pummeled out of existence.

"So what's the worst of it, Dr. Shecter?" Rockson asked as the rest of the top science, military and intelligence brass of the city listened intently.

"Well, we've thrown everything into a computer as all readings and data are coming back," the white-haired, pipe-smoking Shecter, genius of Century City's futuristic projects, said. Over the last thirty years, invention after invention had spewed out of him. People depended on Shecter for solutions. "We already know the medical casualties. Out of a population of what was last recorded at 45,678, we have at least nineteen thousand dead and another ten thousand wounded. The rest of the population is in basically good shape . . ."

They all shook their heads for the hundredth time since they had met to figure out what to do about the future of Century City.

"But in its own terrible way, the loss of equipment—though it's cruel to say it—is even more of a catastrophe," the chief scientist went on to say, with total surety in his voice. "The quake ripped our power generators, and our transmission equipment has been cut to shreds. Connectors, coils, magnets, all ruined. We're running on emergency right now," he said, "for the hospitals, air pumps, pure water and a few other vital areas. Otherwise the city is virtually in the dark. To get C.C. functioning again must be our priority number one objective. My computer men can draw up a list of needed supplies and we can send to the neighboring free cities for—"

"I think we should devote our main energies to defense," General Trasner spoke up firmly from across the dust-coated conference table, which had been set up in a meeting room that had been cleared of debris. "We're extremely vulnerable right now. If attacked by anything from Reds to cannibal hordes, we would have some real problems."

"Medical is the first priority," Surgeon Landers raised his voice. "I must represent the sick and wounded who need constant attention, blood transfusions, food . . ." They all began speaking at once, until Rockson spoke up, his voice booming over theirs for a moment. Although each man had an ego as big as the sun, all deferred to Rockson. The Doomsday Warrior was a name known throughout America; he was the shining hope for the starving masses at the mercy of the Reds. His presence was no less powerful in real life as it was in the growing legends around his deeds.

"Let's first assume that all our needs will be met to the extent that they can," Rockson said. "As military commander of the city and top-ranking man in command—in the President's absence, I can guarantee that with help from other cities." He felt that his voice would be for the moment the guiding one. "But Dr. Shecter's right. It's energy that runs a city; without it this whole place is just a cave. And it will only get worse without power. Without power, we're back with the animals."

"Exactly my point," Shecter said, banging his pipe down hard on the table so their heads all jerked nervously. "We can't sustain this place, perform the necessary medical treatments or keep our defenses without power. Already we've lost a lot of information on computer. There were dupes of some of it, but information that took many years to develop is irretrievably gone. Much of the city's internal structures and foundation are in danger of further collapse as well, unless vital support work is done—foundations, beams put in. That requires power for charging the battery-powered heavy moving and lifting equipment. Those that weren't crushed, that is."

Rockson raised his hand, a deadpan look on his grime-encrusted face. "We were up in Pattonville not too long ago and found a huge supply depot there. I put it in the report delivered to Rath and your R.D. boys. It was filled with some heavy stuff, even bulldozers, and acres of shelving filled with every damn thing you'd need to rebuild a city. Lots of electrical conductors; cables too; and generator parts," Rock said, looking at Shecter expectantly.

"Then let's do it," Dr. Shecter said, banging his palm with a thunderous slap on the table, sending up a little cloud of dust that hadn't quite been cleaned off. It seemed to wake everyone up to 100 percent, as eyes flew open from the sound, all of them fearing for an instant that another quake had struck.

"I propose that Rockson gather an expeditionary force of men and hybrid pack teams, head to this supply depot at Pattonville and get their asses back here quick." Shecter said this firmly, without any further ado. There was a time for debate, and a time for just doing it!

"There are only about fifty good combat-hybrids in the stables right now," Ingersall, head of supplying all outside missions, spoke up nervously. "A lot got killed in the quake. A lot were taken out in recent missions as well. It hasn't been a good year all around," he said with a sardonic edge in his voice. "This would leave us nothing more than a few dozen combat 'brids in fighting trim for other missions and emergencies. Besides, the whole city should vote on—"

"No!" Shecter spoke up, slamming his pipe again as if showing he couldn't stand equivocators. "A man has to know what to do, and then do it. The ceilings are falling down! There's no time."

"The Good Doctor and our esteemed Mr. Rockson are right," Colonel Rath spoke up. The hawk-nosed man was head of security and intelligence in the city. He and Rockson had often not gotten along, to say the least. But they respected each other. And now Rath was on Rock's side! "We're not going anywhere! If someone attacks us . . . we'll damn well fight our asses off from here. There's too many wounded, too many potential disasters waiting to happen all over C.C. for us to evacuate at this moment. It's out of the question. Anyway, there are several hundred hybrids of lesser stock, the kind that do loading and transport work. So, it's not like there'll be nothing with four legs left in this miserable wreck of a place!"

"Well, I guess this is still a democracy even if we're in Red Mode trouble," Rockson spoke up. "So I know everything will go much better if we vote on it, rather than my commanding it! As C.C.'s top military officer, you all know I am mandated by Constitution to take the power if I have to."

They voted quickly and 43 to 7 agreed to send Rockson's team to Pattonville.

"Thank you for your confidence," Rockson said, meeting each of their eyes for an instant as he looked around the table.

"Then it's settled," Dr. Shecter said with a grin and a soft clap of his hands together. The man knew how to make pleasant noise when he wanted to. "I guess, without being pushy, you'll be leaving in the morning," Shecter said, looking at his watch.

"Yeah, I should be able to get some sort of squad together with my usual team of officers heading it with me. Supplies will be the hard part. Light and fast is how we must travel."

"Just give me a list by midnight—I'll have it all for you by six in the morning," The Quartermaster,

Higgins, spoke up. "That's a promise."

"Okay then, I'm going to head out of this meeting and the rest of you can work out your end of this mess. We'll do the best we can, push the 'brids to their limits— and ourselves to our limits. That's a promise." Rock turned and walked out, down the rubble-strewn corridor. He made a brief surveillance of what was occurring now in the city. Using the three working mini-dozers that had escaped destruction, and sheer arm power, citizens formed long lines and passed debris into large piles in the central square, to be used or thrown out later. Rockson felt these people were the most courageous and uncomplaining people he'd ever known. His people. And not for the first time since the day he'd walked into the city as a frightened teen fleeing from the death of his family, Rockson felt like he belonged, and he had pride to be part of them all.

Two of the levels had been cleared, though the dust lingered everywhere.

He gathered up his elite squad who were still doing search and rescue op's all over the city and told them of the mission. The men at first seemed reluctant to give up their searching, as there were clearly others still buried in hell-holes of collapsed rock and cement. But Rockson told them that their journey was the most important mission there could be for the city.

He at last had his whole unit together: Chen, the martial arts master of the city, maybe even a better fighter than Rockson, though the Doomsday Warrior had never put it to the test. Detroit, the ebony-faced Freefighter who wore a bandolier of grenades. McCaughlin, the big Scotsman who was a deceptively strong and fast fighter beneath his outer folds of fat. Archer, a near giant with the strength of five men. And Sheransky, the newest member of the team, a Russian defector who had already proved his loyalty, and smarts, more than once.

"You dudes will have to do more than just combat duty this time round," Rockson addressed them as they stood among the ruins. "We'll be bringing thirty men with us. But they're not exactly used to this kind of mission outside the city. They're green as fresh trees for what we're going to go through to get way over to Pattonville. So that means that each of us will be responsible for eight to ten men. I want them organized. Keep on them. I want no casualties."

"Yeah, okay, Rock," a few voices spoke up.

"OFFFICCCEEERRR," Archer said with his finger on his mouth, as if the idea held infinite possibilities. The others looked at each other and laughed heartily.

"Hey, men, Archer *will* be an officer on this mission! All kidding aside, the guy knows every leaf and punji-stick trap, every killer animal's scent. He'll scare the shit out of the recruits too, that's for sure. They won't have time to get scared about whatever tries to eat us. So go easy on Archer—understand?" He looked at them hard, as there wasn't time to play around at all.

"Understood," they answered, with a little more enthusiasm this time.

"Then I want you all to get it together. You've five hours. Quartermaster Higgins will help you with outfitting the raw recruits. But as you can see—it's speed, men. This mission is going to be a blur. We'll meet at the North Chamber prep-stable at 0600. Catch the early light, get a good move through the mountains. Questions?"

"No sir," Chen said firmly for all gathered. "We all know how to proceed. You go do what you have to."

Rockson saluted them to show they were on military time now and they returned the gesture. Even Chen, who was second in command. He gave Rockson the role of leader on all combat missions. Back in the city, they were equal, according to the latest council rules. But when moving fast and deadly, there could only be one chief.

"Rockson?" a young, pimply man came running up almost as soon as Rockson hit the corridor, while the rest of the team tore-ass in all directions to prepare.

"Yeah," Rock replied as he watched the puffing teen who was doing messenger duty between different rescue operations. Much of the intercom and other communications equipment were out.

"Message from Dr. Shecter! Please see him immediately in Level 14—the test chambers."

Rock made his way up the ramp system to Shecter's science lab level. The signs that pointed out the way to the various floors and functions of Century City were mostly down, though a few hand-lettered ones had been hastily put up. Still, just about everyone who lived in C.C. knew where everything was, by the time they were six. The directions were more for outsiders—tourists!

"Ah, so glad you could make it," Dr. Shecter said, as Rockson came into his office. "I know you've sure as hell got a week's worth of prep to do overnight."

"Right on that," Rock replied. Shecter was the only man on earth he would have gone out of his way to see at this moment, as a matter of fact.

"How's the foot?" the head scientist asked, looking down at Rockson's slight limp.

"Not too bad," the Doomsday Warrior replied. "Got it all taped up, another antibiotic/pain shot. I'll be okay. Mutants heal well."

"Well, some of my advanced med and field crew— and myself, I must add—have come up with something for you, Rockson. A few finishing touches and—presto voilà." He pulled a pair of strange-looking boots from the side of his desk and slammed them down on the top. "We got your foot measurements from med—and made the heels and soles a little more symmetrical. So, you should have more symmetrical balance, even with the cast on." The cast was only a half-inch thick, but Rockson had been feeling the off-centeredness of it. He knew it wasn't good to show the slightest bit of weakness in the wasteland. The weak, the wounded, they were the ones attacked first.

Rockson sat in the chair on the other side of the desk and tried them on. The boots felt good, snug and strong, like his usual field boots. He stood up and walked around.

"They feel damn good. How about the rest of the team?"

Shecter coughed and rose up a bit unsteadily with the aid of a cane which he used these days. The man was getting on. Rockson was going to miss him, more than he dared admit. In many ways, Shecter had been his mentor, his teacher, his—father.

"My field tech crew is loading up the mission force with every goddamn bit of junk we've been able to salvage: synth-medicines, reflector blankets, instafood, liberator rifles and, ammo-up-the-diodes! You send one of your men around here later and—"

"Okay, okay, doc," Rockson laughed. "I'll get the lowdown in your brief! Thanks, Mr. Einstein," he said. "Hang in there, pal, keep everyone digging. I'll be back faster than a rad snake can take down a rat. And thanks for the kill-boots."

Chapter Five

They left on the dot of their departure time; the force of thirty-five and Rockson. A whole shitload of 'brids tethered together sent up a cacophony of braying as they came into the purple-dawned sky from the gray shadows of C.C.'s embarking chamber, squeezing one at a time through the camouflage-slit.

"Take it slow," Rockson yelled back from his lead 'brid, Snorter, probably the fastest animal in the city. "And that goes for the rest of you," he said firmly, glancing around hard at Chen, Detroit, McCaughlin, and Archer, who were keeping a sharp eye on the unit's men. Sheransky took up the rear of the trail. The blond Russian was paranoid enough to think something was going to leap from behind every tree.

Rockson could see that the recruits were excited, their eyes wide with fear, but also full of good humor. They all smiled and looked more like kids on a picnic than grown men about to engage in the battle of their lives. Rockson knew at least half of them weren't coming back. Those were the odds. The Doomsday

Warrior felt responsible for every one of the fuzz-faced, unkempt Freefighters. They were as green as you could get. Slow, they'd start out real slow. Rock would let everyone calm down, the 'brids too, and then he'd build up a little speed. But he vowed to keep a tight grip on this whole hastily assembled force. It was too unwieldy already with the 'brids' wandering out of line, the men not really concentrating on danger as they breathed in the thick, pungent perfumes of the pines and gazed around as wildlife went rushing through the brush.

It was a beautiful morning, and a clear one. There was just a band of thin green strontium clouds high above, that shimmered like the rings of Saturn. One of the legacies of the old world, a remnant that its atomic fires had left behind for man to deal with, even a hundred years later. Rockson had pretty much grown used to the rings of radioactivity in the upper atmosphere. But this one looked meaner, more vibrant and glowing than most he'd seen. He spun around in his saddle for the tenth time in the last two minutes to check the men.

"Relax, Rock," Chen, riding behind him, said as he caught the Doomsday Warrior's nervous face. "The men are sitting tight on the newbies."

"Green is green, Chen." Rockson replied with a snort. "We'd better keep an eye on them, and that includes you, or there will be a few missing by tonight."

"Gotcha, Rock," Chen said, shutting up. He could see his field commander wasn't exactly in the friendliest of moods.

Rock's eyes were bloodshot, barely open. He hadn't slept since the collapse, and his body and mind were begging for rest. But they'd barely begun the journey.

There wouldn't be sleep until night. His mind drifted back to trying to get a snore or two in one of the emergency sleeping chambers, a whole half floor of which had escaped the holocaust. It must have been three in the morning that Rona had come in. Just like that; no knock, no nothing. And she was all over him right away. Like a wildcat in heat. She just didn't want to let go.

It seemed to be like this more and more, as Rona just couldn't bear to let him go off on another mission where the probabilities grew higher with every departure that he wasn't coming back. Not that he could blame her. She wanted to be his wife, have a child. She'd told him that fact again, whispering in his ear as they had made love. . . .

"Rock, look out," Chen screamed out, pulling the Doomsday Warrior from his erotic reveries atop the half-ton animal. Rock suddenly saw a huge branch coming in at chest level. It would take him down like a bowling pin hit by a death ball. Rockson's senses were suddenly on full alert as he swung himself fast down over the 'brid's right side, hanging there like a trick rider. They passed safely under the tree as Chen and the others had the troop ride around the thorned branch of the rare "Swat-Elm." A tree that disliked people coming too close. It was one of the many nasty mutations from the Great War's radiation.

"Sorry about that," Rockson said sheepishly, as Chen came riding up after they'd all passed around it. "I was, uh, thinking—"

"Come on, Rock," Chen said with a narrow grin. "You just gave us all this big lecture on survival out here. And then you're in dreamland. Let's get it going.

41

You of all people should know there's no time for dreaming." Chen was playful but there was an element of seriousness. Rockson was in just too important a position to allow his concentration to slip, not for even one moment. Rock got the message and took a cold swig of water and then two mega-caffeine pills. Within minutes, he swore he could feel the caffeine moving through his blood and sort of opening his eyes a little wider, making his brain feel like there was something going on inside.

The crystal blue morning filtered down through the towering fir forests all around them as the birds went wild, chirping and cheeping up a storm as if they were enjoying the crisp, clear beauty in their own feathered way. The convoy had already made good time, all things considered, and Rock started relaxing just slightly. He always felt tense at the beginning of a mission; the preparations made him nervous, afraid he'd forget something. But once out in the wilds, his mutant nature took over and he was just a tightly coiled system of muscles and perceptions on the alert.

But his mood changed drastically when they came to a series of narrow trails that he had used for years to get down out of this section of the Rockies. The pathways were now virtually wiped out, whether by avalanche or washout from the rains he didn't know. And it hardly mattered what the cause was, for Rock knew that without the trails they would easily add a day or more to the journey—by having to crisscross all the way around this mountain.

"Shit," he muttered to himself as he held up his arm, bringing the force to a lurching stop. He motioned for Chen and Detroit to come forward. The Freefighters atop their 'brids soon looked down over the long slope below with their commander.

"What do you think?" Rock asked, looking down at the snow-sprinkled decline.

"About what?" Detroit asked with a snort.

"About us going down that way," the Doomsday Warrior replied. The other two grew a little pale. "The 'brids have been trained for that kind of descent," Rock said, knowing the words didn't sound all that convincing. "We'll just lose too much damn time if we take the Western route." The men looked down, surveying the almost forty-five degree angle drop that looked like it went down a good mile.

"Unfortunately I think you're right," Detroit spoke up first, shaking his head slightly from side to side.

"Let's move, Rock," Chen chimed in. "We just don't have the time to waste a day or more. I'm with you on this one. There are too many people back at C.C. waiting desperately for our return." Although Rockson was the leader of all combat missions, he wasn't infallible. The advice of his top men was extremely important to him and he listened to it much of the time. He probably would have decided yes anyway in this case, but it helped to have his officers agree with him.

"All right, men," Rockson said, sitting high on his saddle and addressing the rest of the unit. "We're going to do a little butt-sledding, down this snowy slope here." The recruits looked at each other with fear in their eyes. They glanced down the long, steep, snow-strewn slope like it was the last thing they'd see. "So, I want you to tighten up the gear on your 'brids. All saddles and junk should be firmly in place. My officer-team will go around to make sure you got it right. We'll

43

send the pack-'brids down first. They've all been trained for this," Rockson didn't add that some of them, the newer ones, hadn't. "You'll come down behind them to avoid getting crushed, if one of them goes over."

It took about fifteen minutes for them to get everything prepared and then the 'brids were led to the edge of the descent. Rockson had Snorter go first. He knew the big steed wasn't afraid of such drops; in fact, it had taken a few before and had seemed to enjoy the challenge. And the hybrid would show the others that they could do it too. The main thing was not to have the 'brids panic on the long slide.

"Go ahead, boy," Rockson said, slapping the animal on the flank. With a surge of its legs, Snorter leaped over the side. It landed on its right side, since it was impossible to stand up all the way down. And immediately it proceeded to slide right down the slope like a sled made of fur and hide. The snow formed enough of a cushion for the animal to avoid scraping itself up on gravel beneath, and the icy sheen allowed for almost frictionless passage. Then the elite team's seasoned 'brids were sent down. Rockson wanted the other untrained 'brids to get a good look at just what was going on before they made their "jumps." The first of them did so neighing and looking pretty uptight. But the animals quickly seemed to understand that staying on their feet wasn't the way to go and they fell into the side-sledding that the ones before them did.

All in all it took about five minutes to get them all going down, giving a twenty-second space between each one in case there was some sort of collision. Then it was the Freefighters' turns. Rockson went first, sliding in a sitting position, with his field jacket tucked under his butt to keep it from freezing up like a slab of ice. He pushed off and a big smile crossed his face. He hadn't sledded for years, but it immediately brought back memories of his teenage years when he and other youth of the city had spent weeks at a time out with real homemade sleds in their mountains. The tear-proof Freefighter pants would hold up. He built up speed, but used his hands to slow a little. Behind him he could hear yelps and laughs as the rest of the team followed close.

Rock flew down the hill like a bobsled without a rudder, his face flushing with the rushing air. Below, he saw the 'brids had already gotten to their feet and were walking around in dizzy circles, waiting for their riders to join them. Rock came down out of snow like a rocket and rolled over a few times as he hit the flatter terrain. He slammed into the side of a 'brid and then rose up, dizzy himself from the exhilarating ride. He had to reach out and steady himself on the 'brid's mane, but after a few moments, he regained his bearings and balance. He looked up the slope and saw the whole crew coming down like bats out of hell. Rock positioned himself by the bottom of the slope and helped stop the men as they came tearing down. The others who reached the bottom quickly joined in and grabbed hold of each man as he rolled down the bottom of the incline.

When all was said and done, everyone accounted for, Rockson was pleased to find that there had been no major injuries among the men. There were plenty of bruises and scrapes, but nothing really bad. Except for one of the 'brids. It had broken a front and a rear leg. It was not going to make it.

If it had just been one leg, they might have tried for an instant-splint and sent it on its way back to Century City, as the animals were trained to wander their way home. But two legs—there was no way it would make it. It was cruel to leave it out here in the woods. Wolves, snar-lions, bears, God-knew-what, all would be out soon enough to see what was cooking.

"Sorry, pal," Rock said, taking out his shotpistol as the hybrid horse lay on its side with a look of intense pain in its big eyes. He lowered the .12 gauge to the side of the 'brid's head and fired just behind the ear. The big steed slumped over into the snow, blood seeping out like a pool of bad luck around its head and neck. Rockson could see the other men, the new recruits, looking at the death scene with anger and fear.

They better get used to it fast, Rock thought. Death was everywhere out here. The 'brid's blood was only the first of much that would be spilled.

Chapter Six

The recruits kept looking at Rockson with a mixture of fear and hostility for the next few hours. The officer-team didn't even think twice about it. They'd seen it happen before and no doubt would again. Several of them had, in fact, had to eat their steeds on past missions when it became necessary. Though they didn't particularly like to talk about it—they all knew that survival sometimes belonged to the ruthless.

Rockson didn't pay attention to the emotions of the green recruits. They might as well get used to it all now, and fast. Things were going to get a hell of a lot worse than a dead 'brid. Death so early on the mission would keep them on their toes. He noted their expressions were already hardening as their eyes swept back and forth across the woods of the lower Rocky Mountain slopes.

They came out of the steeper section of the mountains and down into the foothills. Here the vegetation was harsher, the trees stunted, the wildlife seemed less prevalent. And with the opened skyline

Rockson felt his paranoia fill his chest. For the sky was pulsing with blue and red waves of energy. It was as if the strontium clouds were dropping down and mingling with the unusual aurora borealis. He had seen it many times at night, but rarely in the day. Its irridescent colors looked ominous against the bright daytime sky.

Rock could see that the men were beginning to grow restive. He could hardly blame them what with the frightening light show above. Still, they made good time once they reached the sparse, rolling foothills. The first-day anxiety of the mission had filled the whole team with adrenaline and fueled them along past their fear. As the sun dropped out of the sky, Rockson saw a rise, about thirty feet higher than the surrounding bush-dotted terrain. It looked easily defensible and was wide enough, about a hundred feet across, to bivouac the whole crew.

"Hold up, Freefighters," the Doomsday Warrior said, raising his arm and rising up in the saddle as he turned to face them. It took a good twenty or thirty seconds to get the whole unit stopped.

"We're going to camp out for the night," Rockson addressed them. "Up on that hill. I know the first day was hard, especially on the butt." The men laughed, happy to feel their mouths move in something other than a downward direction. "So dismount and lead your 'brids up the side of this rise," Rock said, pointing toward the flat-topped hill. "Don't need any more injuries—at least on the first day," he added sardonically. He knew he could have ridden Snorter up, but there was no sense in showing anyone else up. He jumped down from the saddle, and taking the reins of

48

the big mount, led him slowly up the medium-steep slope. The steed made it easily without slipping. Though many of the recruits seemed to have a little trouble with theirs, as the animals stumbled and made quite a storm of dust and sound.

But soon they were all up top, and they tethered the hybrids on a long nylon line set up between two pine trees at either side of the hilltop. They took down feedbags filled with the super energy concoction of Shecter's tech-boys. The 'brids slurped the stuff up, not realizing that that was all they'd eat—it was not just an appetizer. But though the bags would leave the animals a little miffed at not having more, the vitamin and energy infused out-like material would give them plenty of strength for days. Before they started really losing any weight.

The men set up their sleeping bags—aluminized outers to protect not just from cold, but also rays. And even with the confusion of the large team, everything was actually more or less together within about fifteen minutes. The men sat around shooting the bull while they rested up their pained thighs and shoulders and butts. Riding for many hours, especially over rough terrain, did wonders for the entire musculature, making a man feel like he had just been thrown into a blender, set on high and left there for a month or two. But they'd toughen up.

They had been in camp about half an hour when Archer came striding up the hill, back from a little hunting in the thicker brush about a quarter-mile off. His huge crossbow that looked like it could take out the side of a tank was over his shoulder and over the other shoulder of the black-bearded mountain man was a small unicorn-like deer creature. It wasn't huge, maybe fifty pounds, but the men let out a cheer as he walked along the plateau. Archer raised the thing up, the huge arrow hole visible in its chest where he had made a perfect strike, and he got a big smile on his face.

"FOOOOODDD," he said, holding it by its single horn like a trophy. Then he got a funny look on his face as he suddenly realized he was supposed to share it with all of them. He walked over to McCaughlin, a/k/a "Cookie," who had set up a small cooking area. Archer dropped it at the man's feet with a look of great pride.

"All right, my good man," the Scotsman said, beaming. "I was going to make some protein soup from dry mix, for the crew—but now I think you've made their day. Mine too," he added with a twinkle in his eye. He lifted the thing and took it to the edge of the rise and began butchering it with a trail-designed laser cutter. Within an hour, as the night turned totally black but for the shimmering magnetic bands of aurora above, they were all sitting around eating a delicious stew of dried vegetables and fresh meat.

After that, they pretty much fell out, crawling into their sleeping bags as Rockson set up a four-man watch at each point of the hill, to be changed at two-hour intervals. When he awoke, the dawn was already cracking open the night's blackness and spiderwebbing down subtle weavings of blue light. For a moment he was pissed off, as he had told Chen to wake him at three to check on the camp. But the Chinese martial arts master walked over even as the Doomsday Warrior was rising up, with a steaming metal cup of McCaughlin's famous synth-brew.

"Sorry," the Chinese Freefighter said with a lopsided grin as he handed Rock the mug. "I didn't wake you because I could see how beat you were. I know you want to keep your hands on every damn thing going on here. But it won't do any good if the commander of the mission falls out of his saddle and splatters his brain all over the place."

"Thanks," Rock said with a smile, as he realized that Chen was right. Sometimes in the name of being the "perfect commander" he pushed his own body too hard, too far. He felt a hell of a lot better than he had the night before. He took a swig of the steaming brew. "Anything happen last night?"

"Not a thing," Chen replied holding his own brew that wasn't coffee but something the Scotsman had made from various powders and herbs that he always took with him on missions. "Detroit and I supervised the guard—and other than a few rustlings around the hill, some animal sniffing out the situation, nothing to report. I'll get the show on the road," Chen said, letting Rockson sit there on his bedding so he could finish his brew.

They set out, the men in a good mood after they had survived their first day. They headed through the bush for about ten miles and then came to a much less vegetated area, a prairie-like terrain that stretched off for as far as the eye could see.

Rock paused at the edges of the plain and took out his field binocs, standing up on Snorter's back to check it out. Nothing threatening, he noted. No earthquake faults or herds of carnivores. He sat down again and motioned the unit forward. Immediately they were slowed to almost half-speed. The 'brids kept sinking

51

down a few inches with each step in the soft, sandy soil. The sun was out with a vengeance today, and after just an hour of riding, Rock had them stop and take out the Shecter survival-suits that had been created just months before to cover their bodies from head to toe. It looked like they were covering themselves in aluminum foil. But though the men laughed and pointed at one another with amusement, they quickly found that the things helped a lot, reflecting back over 90% of the sun's thermal energy. The 'brids didn't need their head coverings—yet. They could stand far more heat and radiation than their human riders. Though, if it got much worse, Rock would make sure he'd cover their skulls as well.

The terrain got deader and deader. And even within the protective suits, the men could feel the searing dry air. They had been out a good four hours with nothing in sight but more of the same when Rockson saw some white objects poking out of the sand about a hundred yards off their due-north route. He headed the team slightly to the right to get a look, and his jaw dropped open as he came up on the objects.

Bones, huge ones at that; a whole field of them stretching for several hundred yards. It looked like a graveyard for giants.

"What the hell?" Chen asked as he came up alongside the Doomsday Warrior who had slowed them to a crawl.

"I'd bet dollars to synth-doughnuts that they're dinosaur bones," Detroit exclaimed, coming up on the side of Rock. "I've read all about 'em. This whole section of country is filled with the ancient lizard bones. There's nothing else that ever lived that had a thigh bone that big."

And indeed, they could easily see, that many of the bones sticking out were huge, far too big for anything alive on earth whether mutated or normal.

The rest of the crew had pulled to a stop as well, as everyone stared down in utter amazement at the acres of bones.

"How old do you think they are?" Chen asked.

"At least sixty million years," Detroit replied with a big grin. "Could be a lot older. Some of these real big boys go back 160, even 200 million years.

"Damn, and cheese goes bad after a couple of days," McCaughlin laughed, as he joined the action at the front of the force.

"Make some soup stock out of that, hey, Cookie?" Detroit said from atop his 'brid, leaning over in the saddle and slapping the Scotsman on the shoulder.

"In Russia—even bigger," Sheransky said with a self-mocking grin. "Takes two or three of them for even one Russian dinosaur." They all stared at the huge leg bones, collar bones and so on. A pickup truck could have driven through the eye of a gargantuan head half-poking through the sun-baked sand.

"Mapman," Rockson yelled out to Peters, a young fellow with concave face and skin still broken out all over with acne.

"Sir!" the youth barked, as he pulled his 'brid up near them and saluted.

"I want you to mark this spot on your map, mister. No big detail, just the basic location and approximate size of the bone field."

"Will do, sir," Peters said, quickly pulling out his grid chart and sextant and drawing in some lines and measurements. Dr. Shecter would be interested in this. He and his boys were always eating up new data that Freefighting expeditions brought in. Trying to reconstruct a picture of the new America. What was of value—and what was of danger.

While they were all staring as the mapper took his measurements, two of the pack-'brids had somehow come free from their reins at the end of the convoy. Without really being noticed by anyone, they made their way around the side of the force and before they could be stopped were walking through the center of the bone field.

"Get those 'brids!" Rock shouted out, seeing the steeds loose. For even as the animals crashed through a mound of huge ivory bones, the things crumbled like they were made of chalk dust. In a flash the two animals were coated with the stuff. Probably would be hard to get the stuff off!

"Who the hell didn't keep an eye on those two?" Rock bellowed out in anger. It was exactly the kind of stupid mistake that would cost them in other, more treacherous situations. He was pissed off too at the destruction of something that had lasted for eons. But in a flash he saw that the hybrid horses were in far more trouble. Suddenly both of them stopped dead in their tracks. They both got looks of surprise on their furred faces and began trembling. At first it was mild, but within a few seconds they were vibrating and jumping up and down as if in an uncontrollable frenzy. Foam poured out from their opened mouths. And, within ten seconds, both had keeled over into the prairie.

Blood poured from their mouths, eyes, ears, and every orifice of their bodies. The shaking grew wilder as they slid around the sand, staining it red. Within a minute they were dead.

"Stay away from them!" Rockson screamed out, as sone of the recruits started to dismount to see what had happened to the 'brids. "Don't go another inch closer! Leave the supplies on them!"

Rockson got them all the hell out of there fast, making a wide circle around the bone field. God only knew just what was inside the decomposing, prehistoric monsters. But he and his team weren't going to be the ones to find out.

He stopped them after going about half a mile on the other side, and gave the entire unit a stern lecture about being extra careful out here. They had seen first hand just what the fates held in store in the wastelands for anything, man or animal, that didn't stay alert at all times.

Chapter Seven

The weather changed dramatically overnight. From bright glaring sun the day before, the sky was now overcast, looking like it was ready for a storm. It was going to be wet; even the 'brids could sense it, neighing nervously as the troopers saddled them up again and stowed all their gear. Rockson was glad to see that they were getting faster at packing than they had been the day before. The recruits were learning. Death is a quick teacher.

"Freefighters ho!" Rockson shouted out, once he saw that everyone was up in the saddle. He held his right arm straight up and let it drop forward. There was no real need for that kind of stuff, the Doomsday Warrior knew, but men need symbols and a regimen. It gives them strength, makes them feel like a fighting unit.

"What's the plan, Rock?" Chen asked as he rode up alongside the Doomsday Warrior.

"Plan is—we ride til we get there—then we stop." Rockson replied with a twinkle in his mismatched aqua and violet eyes. "It won't be that easy, to say the least. How are your men?"

"Not bad—considering," Chen replied, glancing around at Rock's words to his eight charges, who rode yards behind, two abreast. They plodded through the increasingly hard-packed surface of the long prairie.

"Considering what?" the Doomsday Warrior shot back as he took a swig of water from his canteen hanging on one side of Snorter's saddle horn.

"Considering that half this unit, make that three quarters, has never been on a real mission before. Most of them haven't even been out of C.C. for more than a few days—meat gathering, repairs on external systems, but—nothing heavy duty."

"Well, keep a close eye on them," Rock replied. "'Cause I have a feeling in my mutant guts that it's going to get heavy real fast."

Chen returned back to the lead of his little group of charges. As if Rockson's words had been heard by the very skies, the cloud line, which had grown thick and dark with shadows moving through them for miles, began dropping. Within minutes he could see the rain line about six miles ahead coming straight toward them. It was amazingly straight along the edge, probably the dividing line between two weather fronts, and it created a blanket of darkness as it swept forward at about twenty miles an hour.

Rock had the force stop and put on the Shecter suits, which were multi-purpose for sun, rain, and snow. And again he was pleased to note that the recruits were moving faster, beginning to understand the need to execute Rock's commands without hesitation.

Only Chen, who had his own ninja-type outfit on,

58

didn't put the suit on. He just put on a wide-brimmed, weird-looking Chinese hat. Archer as well didn't feel the need for a suit. Having lived most of his life in the mountains, before Rockson had rescued him from a quicksand pit, the giant had little need for such accessories. The man had run half-naked with the animals for twenty years.

The rain hit them fast and hard, coming down in sheets of liquid silver and gray. The 'brids hardly noticed, merely snorting their big nostrils every once in a while to clear out any water that had found its way in. With their thick hides and huge manes, they were designed by evolution to withstand much worse than this. But it got pretty depressing for the men. Especially after an hour of the same intense gray downpour.

Detroit began singing a marching song by himself at first. But within a few minutes, most of the team had joined in. It wasn't an opera, to say the least.

It was a dumb ditty, but the singing took their minds off the wet trek and put them all in a better mood.

They rode for about three more hours straight across the flat prairie lands. Rock was concerned that the relatively hard-packed surface of the ground would saturate quickly and start a flash flood that would sweep across the plains. He had been trapped in a few floods in his time. But, apparently, just because the earth was so parched around the area, it just soaked it all down like a dry sponge desperate for water.

And then just as quickly as it had begun, the rainstorm was past them and the skies brightened up again, as if the storm never existed. They broke for a quick lunch, Rockson wanting the 'brids as well as the men to dry out and get some rest. Slogging through the wet soil was hard even on the muscular steeds. And after some vegi-burgers mixed with vitapacks that McCaughlin had cooked up the night before and handed out, everyone seemed in much better spirits.

They rode for another hour or so and then came to a long rise that stretched a good ten miles across their route. It was only about six hundred feet high and rose at an easily ridden grade. The whole unit followed Rockson up the side.

As he reached the top and started across the plateau several hundred feet across, Rockson's jaw dropped in amazement. For stretching out below him, extending at least twenty miles, was a vast jungle valley, filled with thick vegetation, towering trees, and mists.

"What the hell?" Chen exclaimed, as he rode up alongside the Doomsday Warrior. The rest of the troop pulled alongside them. They all looked down, virtually speechless. It wasn't just the size of the low mountain-ringed valley but the dramatic change in terrain. It was a different world in the space of perhaps a thousand feet from one side of the rise to the other. This wasn't on last year's survey maps.

Rock took out his field binocs and swept the area slowly back and forth. The rest of the officer-team joined him, bringing their 'brids up alongside and doing the same, all of them looking, but none of them sure for exactly what.

"How the fuck did something like this get created?" Detroit blurted out as he took in the rain forest below. "I mean in the middle of all this prairie?"

"Probably the ring of hills around the whole damn thing," McCaughlin piped up. "I saw something like this when I was down south about twenty years ago—before I came to Century City—and was a hell of a lot skinnier than I am now. The same configuration—a circle of mountains concealing a low valley. Affects the weather patterns dramatically, catching much more of the moisture of passing clouds than on the outside. "Still," he went on as he continued his own sweep with his glasses, "this one is a hell of a lot more steamy than the one I saw."

"What do you think, Cap?" Sheransky piped up, a few 'brids down from Rockson.

"I think we head down into Jungleland," Rockson replied, putting his glasses back in their case. "I don't even see the stinking end of it. It could add days to this trek to start trying to divert and find the flatlands again. It doesn't look great down there—but I do see what look like some fairly passable trails." He looked around at the other officers for their opinions, and all nodded in the affirmative. Rock was the boss. His mutant senses were something they had all learned to trust.

"Okay, men, we're heading down into the greenery. Be alert—because any maneater or whatever the hell's down there waiting for us is going to have a lot more cover than what we've just been passing through." There were nods throughout the team as the men checked their Liberator autofire rifles to make sure they were ready for action.

Rock started down the far slope, moving very slowly as he always did when entering the unknown. Even as they headed down the five-hundred-foot gentle drop-off, they could feel the air temperature changing dramatically. It felt like it was getting a degree hotter every twenty or thirty feet. The air was moist and thick, and filled with a stench of rot and decay, as well as the aroma of countless plants and flowering species. It was the smell of rich and abundant life, a rare thing in a mostly devastated world.

Once they reached the bottom of the long slope and started carefully in through the outer edges of the thick vegetation, they could see it really was jungle; with thick leaved trees, vines hanging down everywhere. Huge orchids and flowers, the likes of which none of them had ever seen, were everywhere. Bluish mists covered the lower portions of the ground, while bird and animal sounds emanated from every direction.

"Watch out for the ground," Rock yelled back to the men behind him, who passed the warning back. "It looks as soft as quicksand in some spots." The trail they found slowly weaved its way through the trees and seemed safe enough. But around them, sometimes just yards away, the earth was soft enough to take a man or a whole 'brid down.

Rockson suddenly heard a whole chorus of sharp sounds and looked up. Sitting in a tree all along a twenty-foot perch were hundreds of exotic birds. He had only seen such variation of plumage and beaks in picture books of the old pre-war world. Nothing like that should have even existed in this part of the country. The Doomsday Warrior thought he had seen it all in his day, but not this.

"Check it out," Detroit half-whispered, half-shouted up to Rock from about thirty feet behind as the whole troop plodded slowly through the misted terrain, their eyes wide in amazement and some fear. "Up at nine o'clock."

Rock looked up and saw another sight that made his jaw drop open. For scampering all around the branches and vines of the trees were monkeys. Several species he could see right away—from creatures hardly bigger than a cat to some large ones that looked like small gorillas. The creatures barked out warnings to one another but didn't seem particularly terrified of the passing entourage below. They sat and watched, hanging by feet, tails, whatever.

"What the hell is going on here?" Detroit piped in from the back. "There shouldn't be anything like this in this part of the world."

"It's here," Rockson replied, turning his head around. "The evidence is before our eyes." And as a dropping plopped right down on his shoulder, the evidence was more than just visual.

"Man down!" a voice screamed out from near the end of the expeditionary force, and all eyes turned as one.

It was like something out of man's worst nightmare. Only this was real. The very last Freefighter on the line was being dragged right up off his hybrid into the trees by a snake. This was no ordinary snake; the thing was a good twenty, perhaps thirty feet long with a body as thick as a beer keg. The trooper's head and chest had already disappeared inside the creature's immense jaws and his legs kicked wildly as the beast pulled him right up into the vines and lower branches of the trees.

Some of the troopers took out their Liberators and began firing until Chen ordered them to stop. The snake slithered through the vines and leaves about twenty feet above them all with amazing speed, shimmering gray and black coloration undulating like pieces of shined metal.

The 'brids couldn't follow where the thing was heading, as it was too thick with foliage, but Rockson, Chen, and Detroit leaped down from their mounts, yelling out for the rest to stay behind. They went tearing after it on foot.

It was a difficult pursuit, as the three Freefighters could hardly see the thing through the trees above. It moved quickly, still holding and slowly swallowing the man. The Freefighters had to leap and jump from log to log, to avoid the thick dank pools of bog-tar that lay everywhere like traps waiting to take them down. The tropical forest seemed to grow wild with excitement, as monkeys howled and birds screamed out choruses of fear.

It took the three of them nearly a quarter mile to catch up with the huge beast. It must have thought it had lost whoever was pursuing it for it stopped on an immense branch, wrapped its tail around it a few times and gulped down its meal for real. When Chen reached it, stopping about fifty feet away, all he could see was the unfortunate trooper's feet sticking out.

Rock pulled out his shotpistol, aiming up toward the head of the snake, but Chen told him not to shoot. He whipped out two starknives, and eyeing the target, suddenly released both of them. One got the thing near the end of the tail, the other starknife Chen threw hit about midsection of its fat serpentine body.

There were two muffled explosions as the plastique-filled starknives ripped the thing open. The snake uncoiled like a worm on a hook and fell the forty feet to the ground. The Freefighters rushed over to it, and Rock jumped on top of the neck as blood spewed everywhere. He pulled out his Bowie knife and slammed the blade into the thing's skull over and over, making sure he didn't push it too deep, so as to avoid hurting the victim who had now disappeared completely inside. They could see the outline of the man in the first six feet or so of the snake.

It continued its death throes, the lower half of the body just bloody shreds from Chen's deadly toys.

"Cut him open," Rock exclaimed, as he started slicing from the mouth down while Chen started up from about eight feet below. It took them only a minute to cut through the thick, bloody guts and scaled skin. And both men, as much horror and death as they had seen, found it hard to keep from vomiting. For as they cut, the remains of the trooper came pouring out. The snake must have had a digestive system like pure acid.

The Freefighter had only been inside its slimy gullet for several minutes at most—but there was nothing recognizable as human that poured out when they finished cutting. Just bones, and a bloody mud that oozed out, joining the snake's own pulsing innards.

The two Freefighters stood up, as Detroit stood a few yards back, his black face turning pale. He'd been covering with his rifle.

"God," Rockson said, looking down at the mess of human being and snake all mixed together. The three of them couldn't tear their eyes away even as they wanted to run off. It was just about the most vile sight any of them had ever seen. Above them, crowds of monkeys and birds all stared down in noisy witness to the theater of death. And as the three Freefighters began walking away, their heads bowed, the animal army above descended to enjoy the feast.

Chapter Eight

"Mount up, men," Rockson said as he and the unsuccessful rescuers returned to the other Free-fighters. They all had looks of fear on their faces. Seeing one of their buddies ripped off like he was an insect had done something to them.

"He's dead all right," Rock said, addressing the unit as they sat up on their 'brids in a semicircle around him. "He went out fast. That son-of-a-bitching snake had digestive fluids like acid. I'm sure he was dead within seconds." The Doomsday Warrior lied, for he had seen that the poor bastard's feet were still flailing around after several minutes.

"Everyone face toward the jungle there, where he lies, and give a moment of silence for a fallen comrade. Even though Andrews didn't get to engage in battle—this was his last battle. He gave his life for his comrades, his city." They all stared at the greenery. Ordinarily, it might have appeared beautiful with its lushness of fruits and flowers. But now it was a killer. A monster-in-green ready to take any of them out.

The silence wasn't long. "Amen," Chen stated softly, after a bare ten seconds.

"All right! Let's get the hell out of here," Rock shouted as he started forward. "Andrews is dead, let's not allow ourselves to follow him. Look out, you hear me? Anything that moves, any shadows, shoot first and ask questions later." He pushed Snorter forward, searching for the narrow trail which was a dry way through swampland on both sides of it.

They rode for about half an hour, getting deeper into the wet greenland. The animal life was profuse. There were frogs, ducks, and the several species of monkeys, many of which followed along swinging through the trees in big groups, curious as to these new invaders into their domain.

Rockson kept seeing snakes too, slithering, not appearing afraid of them. Here and there further off in the brush he saw just the edges of tails or long, flapping tongues that made him know there were other snakes bigger than the one that had gotten Andrews. He gulped hard and tried not to think a hell of a lot about it all.

They had gone on a good hour when they came to a series of low, rolling hills covered with fields of fruit, nectarines, huge golden apples.

"Jumping pack-meals," McCaughlin laughed out from the line. "What do you think, Rock? Let me test a few for poisons, then we can load up. Fresh fruit'll make the men damn happy over the next few days!"

Rockson deliberated for a moment. They needed a rest for a few minutes anyway, the jungle trekking was hard work on the 'brids.

"Sure," Rock said with a grin. Real outdoor fruit. Some of the men had never had anything but the hydroponically grown kind within Century City's artificially lit agricultural levels. Rockson had eaten fresh fruit here and there in his travels. The taste was totally different.

"You two, come with me," McCaughlin said to two of the recruits, who jumped down immediately from their saddles. He walked over about twenty feet to the nearest of the trees lush with large, red globe-like fruits. Taking out a small needle about as big as hypodermic, he poked it into one. Wires in it ran out to a device—the Poison Detector—another one of Shecter's field-engineering miracles.

"These are fine," McCaughlin said as he did an instantaneous sampling of the juices and read out the digital moving letters across a mini-screen on the small computer/monitor. The device was small enough to hold in his hand. "Take as many of these as you can carry in these bags. We'll throw it all on the extra 'brid." He knew it was cruel in a way to talk of the dead man's hybrid so quickly after his demise. But the dead weren't hungry. It was the living who had to go on.

He walked on and sampled another fruit, this one green and long. He poked the needle in again and the digiscreen read out, CITRUS—ACIDIC, BUT ED-IBLE. DO NOT EXCEED TWO IN 24-HOUR PERIOD.

"Take just a few of these," McCaughlin pointed out to the other recruit who was standing alongside him. The big Scotsman's face was absolutely beaming with joy at the thought of what he could do with such culinary treasures in his recipes. The men would eat like kings for the next week, that was for sure. No need for the vitamin C pills to ward off scurvy.

"Here you go, Rockson," McCaughlin laughed like a Santa Claus who'd just gotten a shipment of gifts. "Have one."

Rock leaned down from Snorter as the Freefighter held up his plastic food storage bag. The Doomsday Warrior reached down and took a green and a bluish colored fruit and took a bite of out it, thinking maybe perhaps it was some immense blueberry, his favorite fruit. The juices had barely reached his tongue when Detroit shouted out. Tried to shout anyway, as his voice croaked halfway through. "Look Rock, we're—we're surrounded—"

Rockson froze, his chewing lips in midstride. And he turned to where the ebony-skinned Freefighter was pointing. Coming out of the groves of jungle trees—with their blankets of rainbow fruits was a mini-army of men, and crawling alongside all around them—snakes. Hundreds of the slithering reptiles. All sizes—from tiny ones, up to over ten feet and a few as large as twenty. Rockson was so struck by the force arriving that he just sat there holding the fruit an inch from his mouth. There were about fifty of the men. Rock suddenly saw through the dappled shadow and light streaks of the jungle, as the sun worked its way down from high above, that they were wearing snakeskins, cut to size into pants, vests, jackets. Over their heads were rounded, tight snakeskin hats as well, every one a different color.

Suddenly there were more men coming from the other side of the fruit forest—and then behind them, as Rock suddenly turned in the saddle. In the space of a bite of fruit they'd been virtually surrounded.

"Weapons out, men," Rock screamed as the ad-

70

vancing force now grew truly alarming. Rockson could see that the snakemen were holding long double-headed spears on long poles. They kept prodding the snakes, which slithered all around their feet, but the snakes never even tried to bite any of them. And Rockson could hear a faint crackling sound each time as a snake was touched. The snakemen's spears didn't enter their flesh, just poked them and released a blue spray of sparks. The men were controlling them all, like goddamned dogs on an electric leash.

By the time Rockson had gotten his shotpistol out and was wondering where to start, he saw that they were completely cut off. There were hundreds of the snakeskin-clad men, and more trained snakes than Ted Rockson, or any of them, would have wished to see in ten thousand nightmares. The entire terrain for an acre around them was a slithering pool of hissing snakes, all eyeing them with most interested orange and red eyes. It was the tongues that got to Rock as he froze with the shotpistol, not sure what the hell to do: tongues so long and forked, slapping out fast. They made a sickly wet sound as they flew back in and out.

"What the hell do you think, Rock?" Chen asked, from several yards behind. "As fucked up as this whole scene looks—we don't know if they're hostile. Remember your Anthro lessons back in C.C.," the Chinese Freefighter said. "Never assume hostility—no matter how weird some races may appear—unless they actually attack."

"Yeah, right," the Doomsday Warrior said, with a snort. He was wondering how the hell the man could even have an iota of humor in him at a time like this. But he held his fire and held his left arm up, the signal for the others to hold fire until Rock decided otherwise. The recruits atop their 'brids were trembling, their eyes wide. They held their Liberators, ready to deal out hot lead. Not that any man had the slightest belief that he had one chance of surviving if this crew came in, fangs a-snapping.

Suddenly a huge man came up to within about ten feet of Rockson and stopped. He was a truly formidable-sized fellow, about six-foot-seven with his bizarre outfit of snakeskin sewn together in all sorts of geometric patterns: crosses and circles and squares. He had a large gourd around his neck and pulled it forward, gripping it with both hands. The snake-general, or whatever the hell he was, blew hard on the device and an unearthly noise came out of it. Rockson had heard the sounds of Tibetan Dharma-Horns on an old video of the Himalayan monks once, and it sounded a lot like that. A thunderous bass sound seemed to ripple up his very backbone. The 'brids were nervous as hell and kept fidgeting around, but most of them stayed under control, a testament to C.C.'s stable-hands' good training.

The snakemen and their reptile invasion force came to a stop around the Freefighters. The headman held up his conch and for a moment there was a bizarre silence which settled over everyone, man, hybrid, and snake.

"Stop!" the snake chief shouted out, holding the conch horn high to the sky.

"I am stopped," Rock replied loudly, but without anger. At least the bastard spoke English. One word anyway. "We come in peace, and mean no harm," the Doomsday Warrior went on, letting his pistol slip

72

down into the holster, so the man could see it. Rock knew they didn't have the slightest chance to take on this whole army. It was ridiculous without anything short of a field-nuke.

"Go where?" the snakeman asked, as Rock saw he had three small snakes wrapped around his right shoulder. Clearly a symbol of rank, he realized instantly, as the creatures were dead, and hung as decoration there.

"Going through this land to get to supplies in the north that we need for our village, Century City." Rockson looked hopefully at the guy, like the name might ring a bell.

"Never heard!" the snakeman said, as he walked around Rock and his 'brid. He seemed fascinated, as the others did, by the big steeds. Apparently, though they had everything from chimps to man-eating snakes in this murderous paradise, they didn't have horses or any mammal this big. The snakes didn't seem to take a huge interest in the 'brids; they were just too big for even the twenty-footers to take down. But they sure as hell looked interested in the riders. Rockson remembered just where his pistol was, visualizing the route to it as he spoke.

"They're called hybrid horses," Rockson said with as much friendliness as he could muster. The snakeman reached and stroked Snorter's flank and the big 'brid made a deep sound, pulling back and rearing up.

"Whoa, easy boy! He doesn't mean to offend you," Rock said as he brought the 'brid back down under control. "He's just shy—like that with everyone." The snake-general stepped back a few feet and Rockson could see in his eyes he wanted to take them out.

But, just as quickly, the darkness went out and the snake-general spoke again. "You come! Take to King Bailey. He will decide!" He blew the conch again, and the whole trained-snake-and-snakeskinned infantry turned the opposite way, back toward the direction they had come. Two long lines went down each side of the Freefighters, who were barely able to keep their 'brids from bolting. And they were led off through the groves of fruit trees into the mists ahead, surrounded on both flanks by a blanket of the writhing snakes.

Chapter Nine

They were marched into an area of well-cultivated fruit groves, which lasted perhaps two hundred yards. Then they came to another extremely swampy area. In fact, all of it was surrounded by swamp, extending out at least a mile or more before the mist-covered hills. Rock prayed that these people weren't going to ask him and the rest of the team to swim in that stuff, a surface covered with muck and lily pads and centipedes dancing from rotten ferns to bloated dead fish.

But as they reached the swampline, where the solid earth faded away he saw a number of large rafts made of sections of tree thirty feet long and lashed together with twisted vines. They were marched up to the things, about ten men to a raft, with snake-troopers guarding them and looking them all up and down like they were looking at alien bugs. The snakemen had seen their share of weird nature in their valley—but apparently had never seen other men before, particularly with huge, hairy horse-creatures.

When they were all loaded up onto the rafts, two

snakemen on each side poled into the swampy muck with their long snake-prongs. The things apparently doubled as long push-poles, with the current turned off. The pole-pushers would start at the front and walk down the length of the rafts. It was agonizingly slow going at first, as they pushed off the mud bank. But once they got going and in rhythm, the crafts began picking up a little speed. Nothing to write home about, but a few miles an hour. The trained snakes came right into the watery swamp all around them. It was like the entire herd was a single living entity, so intertwined were the swimming bodies. Rockson wouldn't even think once about diving into that water to escape.

The snakemen pushed the rafts along single file and soon were out hundreds of yards into the swamp. The floral and faunal lifeforms erupted around them in a rainbow of color and jungle screams. The blue mists were low, just a foot or so off the black, thick waters. After another half mile or so, they came to just about the strangest village the Doomsday Warrior had ever seen. Set right in the middle of the black swamp was a huge development of wooden and vine houses built on stilts. They stood on thick foundation logs at each corner and ranged from simple huts with hardly more than a shack on their log-backs, to quite large structures. One house in the center of the three concentric circles of wooden stilts was like some sort of jungle palace. Huge, perhaps a hundred feet from ground to the top, it had levels every twenty feet, each one wider than the next.

As the rafts came slowly into the midst of the village, with enough space between the circles of stilt-dwellings to allow easy passage, Rockson stared in amazement. For men were fishing over the sides of their swamp homes, only they were using snakes instead of poles. Holding one end of what looked like mostly six- to eight-footers, they stood around the edges of the stilt structures on the porches that surrounded all of them. They held the snakes by the tail and then dropped their heads down into the murky depths. It seemed to take only a few seconds to get a strike. The snakes would shake a little and the men would pull them back up— with a squirming fish or frog in their wide-open jaws.

Either the snakes were amazingly well-trained—or had some kind of plugs in their throats! For once they were pulled back up onto the wooden verandas, the snakemen would sort of tickle the reptiles' throats, and the creatures would respond by coughing out the catch. Then the snakes would be allowed to take a few breaths of air—and then sent back under for another catch.

"Wish I had a few of those back in C.C.," McCaughlin said. He was a few yards behind Rockson on the lead raft. Detroit whistled behind him as the whole assault team gulped hard and wondered just what the hell they were getting themselves into. With fruits hanging down from trees and their ability to catch plenty of food out on the porch, Rockson decided the snake-people had it made here. It was like a mini-paradise, with every need provided for and hardly any need to work very hard.

Again, the townsfolk were clearly fascinated by the group of outsiders and their strange animals being ferried in on the rafts. They stood around their fishing platforms where they'd been talking and drinking some kind of beverage from gourds that Rockson suspected was somewhat alcoholic. They all had that slightly bleary-eyed, good-natured look that alcohol brings on. All wore variations of the snakeskin outfits: vests, shirts, pants, mocassins. And the same tight-skinned headdresses. Everything in their lives came from the swamp in some fashion. Rock was beginning to appreciate just how ingenious the swamp folks were.

They were poled up to the huge central stilt-building and then stopped, the rafts pulling side by side until they were held in place by ropes thrown up from the bow and grabbed by snakemen waiting on the nearly hundred-foot-long dock. Ramps were lowered down as the rafts were about five feet below the swamp building's lowest story. Slowly they were led off and then directed about thirty feet. There was a long log and the 'brids were tethered up while Rockson and the rest of the unit's men were led into the great stilt building.

Inside, Rockson could see in a flash that they were in the head-honcho's house. The main room was immense, as wide as the entire structure itself, and at least thirty feet high. Pictures of snakes were everywhere, with skins hanging down from the walls in great tapestries. Snakes, mostly smaller, slithered all over the place, but stayed several yards away from the men, evidently trained to not entangle themselves in the humans' feet. The place had a slightly off-putting smell, a mix of the swamp and muck beneath the building and the scent of so many snakes.

Then Rockson saw the throne at the far end of the great wooden chamber and the extremely large man sitting in it. The wooden and vine chair was equally immense, a good five feet on a side and perhaps ten feet high with a backrest that rose up nearly twelve feet. And woven together on it, in various circular patterns, were a number of snakes with extremely shimmering skins. These were dead, as far as Rock could tell.

The man seemed godlike. He too wore a snakeskin outfit, but his suit was quite elaborate, with teeth hanging all over it, a huge headdress made of small snakes and swamp flowers, and a cloak of purple snakeskin that hung down behind him. On each side of the throne stood a tall guard holding prong-weapons. The headman had his arms folded across his bared chest as he watched the entourage walk in.

"Stop!" one of the guards snapped, and pointed to a bunch of vine cushions that lay in a semicircle about twenty feet from the throne across the wide, wooden-planked floor. "Bow to King Bailey."

The rest of the troopers looked at Rock, not knowing just what to do, as Freefighters in general bowed to no man. But Rockson had been through this before. So they all made quick little bows, most of them never having done so before, and felt strange about it.

"Sit," the guard said brusquely. The dozen or so guards who had led the Freefighters in stood around the sides and came to a sloppy sort of attention. The men all sat down as Rockson nodded for them to obey the command.

"How exciting to have visitors," the headman spoke up from his throne, once they were all seated. "We haven't had any around here for about fifty years. Before I was even born," he added with a friendly enough grin. The snake-king looked around at all of them, as if absorbing their energies. Rockson's men shifted around uncomfortably.

Above them, in some of the cross rafters of the place, snakes, some of these perhaps twelve, even fifteen feet long, slithered around or wrapped themselves around the pieces of branch and looked down like they found the whole scene amusing in some incomprehensible snakish way.

"Why have you come here?" King Bailey suddenly spoke up, his tone changing from one of relative friendliness to one with undercurrents of hostility. "And why have you killed one of our snake-brothers?" For a moment Rockson was confused until he realized the King was referring to the snake they had taken out.

"I'm Ted Rockson," the Doomsday Warrior replied, trying to be as calm and non-threatening as possible. "I am the leader of these men. We were passing through the swamp area here. Didn't even know that there were men living here. I'm sorry for the intrusion. There was a terrible accident in my city, Century City, about two hundred miles to the south. We need supplies and this was a shortcut."

The king looked on with interest, though his eyes didn't reveal a hell of a lot.

"As far as the death of your—brother, I'm sorry about that. It took one of my men and tore off into the jungle. We tried to save him and had to kill the snake. He died anyway." Rockson looked down at the vine and wood woven floor, feeling a surge of sadness for the dead recruit.

"Yes, I see," the king said, as he petted a large black

and gray python that crawled up to him and wrapped itself around his throne and one of his legs. The king seemed to enjoy the snake-fondling, like a man stroking a cat or a dog. "He was a rogue," the head honcho spoke up. "We couldn't allow Mmm-Ptahhh in the camp, as he was constantly after the other snakes and had even attacked one of our own men recently," King Bailey went on. "So you are forgiven on that count. Please do not harm another or . . ." He didn't have to finish the thought, Rockson got the message. The other Freefighters sitting around on the low pillows gulped hard.

"King," Rockson said hesitantly. "May I inquire as to how you speak English so well, how this place came into being, and about your relationship with snakes? I'm not sure that you're aware that this is not exactly how most men live in the outside world."

"Yes, I'll be glad to tell you of our founding," King Bailey answered. "Our ancestors were all part of a traveling circus. 'Barnum and Bailey and Ringling Brothers Traveling Circus and Animal Extravaganza' was the full name. They were heading across this part of the country when the bombs fell. That was that. With their motorized buses and trucks all made useless by electromagnetic pulses, they found this area on foot. It wasn't as swampy as you see it now, but was a protective sanctuary from the radioactive winds and other dangers because of the walls of the great valley. So they settled here.

"At first it was quite difficult to survive, and many of the animals—elephants, horses, many others—died for lack of food. Many of my own human ancestors as

81

well were dead within months. But many survived, and took this whole valley over as their homes. The snakes were released to fend for themselves and the monkeys as well. Both did well here after sustaining losses at the start. All of us learned how to use the environment, how to survive. Snakes are hard to understand, but when you can communicate with them, they're the most loyal of creatures, ready to serve their masters to the death. Now—we live here, there's no need to venture outside. We didn't even know if men still survived out in the wastelands any more. Obviously they do."

"And you—your title is King Bailey, as a symbol of the founding fathers of this great swamp?" Rockson asked.

"Yes," the snake leader said, suddenly pushing the python off his lap, which skittered along the floor and up the wall, finding its own beam to wrap itself around, where it watched the goings-on below. "What do you think of our homeland?"

"I—I—" Rockson began, not even sure what he was going to say, as the story had been so fantastic. But King Bailey cut him off with a wave of his hand. He looked up at the ceiling.

"Please, no more right now. We can talk tonight. We will have a celebration in your honor. We are a rich and generous people. As you may have noticed here already. All of us Ringlings—that's what we call ourselves—are happy. Our needs are provided for. Right now, I have some pressing matters to attend to. Though my people are generally peaceful, there are occasional feuds, even violence. Besides being King

Bailey the V, I also am judge and jury here. Onerous duties! You will be escorted to your own dwellings, and tonight we will talk some more."

The king clapped his hands together. The guards on each side motioned for the men to rise and then led them out of the Royal Swamp Castle.

Chapter Ten

Rockson and his men were brought to another stilthouse about a hundred yards from the last of the outer circle of "Ringling dwellings." It was a large single storey, fortified structure with a vine and leaf thatched roof and no openings except for a heavy door that bolted from the outside.

Why in hell would they need a jail out here? Rockson wondered, after they were herded up a thick ramp to the house and locked inside. He surveyed the place, trying to line up escape possibilities in his mind. They stripped down their 'brids which had also been locked in with them, set up a remuda at one end of the wide stilt-raised dwelling, and put their own gear at the other end.

Suddenly, just as Rockson was completing his walking-tour, there was a commotion and a loud baying. Some kind of huge bee was stinging at a 'brid's nose. Hybrid horses have tough hides, but their noses are less protected. After the tenth or so quick jabbing sting, the 'brid ripped free of its tether, and bolted across the wooden floor. A bunch of the Freefighters reached out to stop it, though it would be almost impossible without the bridle in its mouth. Three of the men went flying onto the stilt-house floor, as the hybrid tore right toward the side as the damn swamp-stinger kept after it.

Suddenly it reached the wall and, without a moment's hesitation, crashed through it with all its strength. The foundation stilts of the prison were only five feet above the water, so the animal didn't fall very far. It landed in the thick scum-blackness of the swamp waters with a loud splash. The creature swam in circles around itself as the bee, satisfied that it made its point, flew off, buzzing arrogantly.

"Here, boy, here," Detroit yelled out from the hole in the wall, trying to guide the animal back. It had just started getting its bearings when something grabbed it from below. The animal's whole body jerked and it got a look of absolute terror on its hairy face. And without another breath, it was pulled down hard and fast.

For a second, Rock thought he saw the predator—a crocodile—this one a good twenty-footer, wide as a barrel, its yard-long fangs around the hybrid's head. Then it was gone, into a low mist that was floating across the surface of the swamp lake.

"Damn," Detroit said. He knew the animal wasn't coming up again.

"Keep a sharp eye on the 'brids, make sure they're tied up tight. And watch your own asses as well," the Doomsday Warrior added with a sharp tone. "If you fall in that—you're dead." Things continued to swim around them, just under the surface as bubbles rose up here and there. Rock could see why no guards were

86

necessary. Nature provided all the escape-proofing the place needed.

He gathered his top men and held a conference at one end of the stilt prison.

"Any ideas?" Rock asked, opening the meeting of Chen, Detroit, Sheransky, McCaughlin and Archer, who he knew didn't understand a lot of what was said, but loved being part of it all.

"Yeah, let's open a pocketbook store," Detroit cracked as he glanced off at the village of the Ringlings, "Alligator bags."

"HAAAATE SNNNAAKKES," Archer groaned out, "AAANDD CROCS!"

"I don't think any of us are too fond of them," Rock grinned. Then his face took on a serious look. "The king seems peaceful. They've let us keep our weapons—not that they would do a hell of a lot of good against a whole swampful of predators. But at least that shows good faith."

"I don't think they give a shit about our weaponry," Sheransky spoke up. "They feel they have the situation in control so totally they don't even have to give it a thought."

"And they're damn right about that," McCaughlin said with a shudder. "I ain't going swimming any time soon." He turned his head to the black foulness that floated below them and then turned quickly away, as he didn't even like looking down there.

"What do you think, Rockson?" Chen asked, not volunteering his own thoughts on the subject.

"We gotta play it by ear," the Doomsday Warrior replied. "It's just too wild a situation to make any plans yet. Keep an eye out for anything that could help us—a boat, a bridge. Try to start memorizing the layout of the village whenever they move us around. You get the message."

"Yeah, Rock," the men replied gruffly.

"And keep a close eye on your squads. One of those guys will go to the side to take a leak—and—and wham, he'll have something with fangs wrapped around his family jewels." The team laughed at that statement, and then split up to check out their charges.

The evening came on fast. One minute sunshine was trickling down all around the vines and monkey-filled trees that stood off from the platform village, the next the place was a chirping and growling darkness. As the blackness descended, eyes lit up the surrounding marshlands. Lanterns, looking like twinkling fireflies, were put on all over the Ringling village. Hundreds of them, so the light reflected off the swampy waters with a bizarre kind of beauty. Within minutes of the collapse of the sun, a raft was being poled over to them. It moved slowly across the slime surface of the swamp, three lanterns, two up front, one in the rear, bouncing around as the Ringlings poled their way patiently along.

"Get on," one of the Snake-men spoke up harshly, as he slammed the raft against the side of the prison-platform. "King Bailey wants the one called Rockson and his top generals. The rest stay." Rock told McCaughlin and Sheransky to stay behind and handle the rest of the fighting force. Both of them could be stern disciplinarians when it came down to it. Rock and the rest of his elite squad loaded up onto the raft and headed out into the sweeping low mists.

All around the raft Rock could hear the snake herds

that apparently accompanied these raftsmen whenever they were deployed. They were headed through the center of the village when the Freefighters heard them—drums, strange rattle-like sounds ahead.

Music, of a sort. The party had begun. They went through the main canal and out the back end. Here was a three storey affair, nearly as nice as the king's own palace. It was lit up all over the place by lanterns which burned some kind of oil.

They reached the side of the party and were led inside. It was a wild scene; a huge balcony swept around the second floor opened up in the center so the king, who sat up there on a different throne, could see all the action at once. And action there was, with feasting, tables filled with numerous kinds of fruit, meat, fish—and snakes. Off to the side, the band now pounded logs in bizarre, shifting beats, shook rattles and blew the hornlike gourds that made screaming sounds.

"Up here," the guard said, probing them with the double-pronged spear poles. Archer growled and the rear guard pulled his pronger back again. They walked up a set of crude stairs and then to the balcony, about twenty feet wide, that ran around the full four walls. It was like some kind of crazy little three-ring circus, snakeskins flapping in the low breeze with jugglers, trapezists, and acrobats.

"Welcome," King Bailey said with good humor as he sat on the throne, a huge table in front of him, taking single bites of things in the hundred-course spread. What didn't taste right he was throwing over his shoulder into the water, where the snakes bubbled around like dogs around a kitchen table and gulped down whatever splashed near them.

"Thank you, your excellency," Rockson replied, with all the sincerity he could muster. "We're all, of course, deeply honored to be your guests." It never hurt to compliment kings.

"The honor is mine," King Bailey said, taking another huge bite of something that looked squirmy and round. Servants in full snake gear came walking in and presented a table full of delicacies to the Freefighters. Sitting down on snakeskin pillows, they dug into the myriad gourd bowls, each filled with a different steaming food, most of them unappealing. Some of the foods were things that looked like brains, and others were membranous masses of various kinds.

Actually most of it was quite good, with flavorings to suit a master chef. Archer kept popping little peach-sized pink things in with gusto, like they were pretzels.

"What are those?" Detroit asked, nodding toward Archer's appetizers.

"Monkey gonads," King Bailey replied, slurping down one of his own. "My favorite, I must confess. Said to make a man virile." The rest of the Freefighters coughed, looked around at each other, and tried to find something on their tables a little less slimy. Below, the music grew ever louder and wilder. Suddenly, from out of the shadows, came a dozen snakewomen. They were clothed in just small swaths of semitransparent skin, and they danced lasciviously around in the center of the wide floor. The horns screamed out insistently and the snake dancers began weaving madly around the room. The Freefighters' mouths froze as they watched the dancers.

"Huh, don't mean to break the wonderful atmosphere here," Rockson said, at the king's side, after about ten minutes. He could see the man was inebriated from the beer-like drink that stood in big mugs on every table.

"No, go ahead, what is on your mind?" the king asked, goofily.

"Hum—you are going to let us leave, aren't you? Because after we sleep off your great shebang here, we have to be on our way. My city is counting on us to return with much-needed supplies. Many men and women's lives, young children by the thousand, depend on us. All will perish, if we should fail to return."

"Of course you can leave, Rockson! Just can't deny a bored king twenty-four hours of company. You can't imagine how dreary it gets around here, with the same faces to look at all the time. Ninety-nine percent of them are not a tenth as intelligent as you. Now, tell me about the outside world. As I told you, my people haven't ventured outside this great valley for a century and more."

Rockson told him what was happening—with the Freefighters versus the Red armies, the mutations, the deserts and earthquake-zones. The king seemed impressed, and the girls down below danced faster. Rockson felt his head begin to swirl from the beer. The last thing he remembered was a dancer straddling a huge snake as the music reached a fever pitch.

Chapter Eleven

Rockson woke up with just about the worst hangover he'd ever had. His skull was throbbing like a pig stuck in a bear trap. He tried to slowly open his eyes, but the dim amount of light that seeped in cut into his skull like a buzz saw on full overdrive. He sat up, not even sure for a few seconds just where the hell he was. It was a dreamlike state that was not particularly pleasant. Then his eyes focused more and the blue sky filtered down through the vines and trees around the island-prison Rock and his men were on. In a flash, everything came back into comprehension, and he remembered he was among the snake people and that he had feasted and drunk enough to keep him in headaches for a year or two.

Around him, other elite Freefighters were groaning. Each man looked pale and a little unsteady, as if his stomach was thinking of sending some of what it had taken in back up again. Even Archer, who could drink down whole barrels of brew, sat up and then rolled over on his side with a lopsided grimace on his bearded face.

"All right, Freefighters," Rockson said, as he stood up. He had to lean against a tree-pole, as he felt as if he might fall over. "Let's get our asses in gear, get some blood in our veins."

The men slowly got up from their sleeping bags and walked around, yawning and stumbling, to their 'brids, tethered at one side of their guest island. They took out food bags and strapped them on to the hybrids' faces, as the animals snapped at them in hunger. There was nothing like a night of no food to make the mutant steeds get pretty ornery.

"How you feeling, Rock?" Chen said, walking over to Rockson, who was making sure Snorter's feed bag was in place as the animal began chewing lustily. "Everyone looks pretty screwed up."

"Yeah, I know," the Doomsday Warrior replied, squinting as the morning sun came down through a wall-slit like a sword into his eyes. "I wouldn't be surprised if we were all drugged last night. But it doesn't make sense. Why not just bump us off? If they slipped something in our food and wine . . . It's as easy to make a man puke as it is to kill him."

"Yeah, that's for sure," the Chinese-American said, handing Rockson a small bottle of something red and strong-smelling. "Not enough for everyone," Chen said, with a smirk. "My personal stock. Just take a sip—it does wonders for hangover—and other ailments. It's my all-purpose, colon-cleansing, mole-removal, fungus-ridder, and snake-bite medicine. Handed down from generation to generation in my family, for the last two thousand years."

"Yeah, right," Rockson said, cynically. But he took

the sip. Chen sure as hell looked a lot better than the rest of them this fine swampy morning. Maybe the stuff worked. He handed it back and looked around. Already the air was getting thick and sultry. A gray fog was hovering over the swamp and crawling up toward the island they were on. Rock could feel sweat starting to well up under his arms and along his shoulders. It was going to be one of those days.

"Okay, men," Rock said, addressing all the men whom he quickly gathered together. "We're going to be pulling out today—hopefully, in a few hours. So get your pissing done and all your gear together. I'm going to have me a little talk with Emperor Snakeface back there." He paused as he thought about how to say the next few sentences, while the men looked on in that kind of bemused expression of someone who doesn't really want to go. Hell, it was pretty comfortable where they were staying. Yet at the same time, the environment was not exactly conducive to good fighters.

"Now, I don't want to give anyone ulcers," Rockson went on, "but I want all your weapons cleaned, loaded, and in firing order.

"If something goes wrong—we damn well better be ready to kick booty to get the hell out of here." That brought some pretty nervous glances to their eyes and their energy level shot up like the mercury on a dying man's thermometer.

"What do you mean exactly by that, Rock?" one of the men spoke up. "Do you have any reason to—"

"Just a feeling," Rockson replied softly, trying to sound more optimistic. "Just a crazy old mutant feeling. Anyway—it's always good to be prepared."

Suddenly, there was a low, splashing sound and they turned to see one of the poled rafts coming toward them from the direction of the Ringling village. Rockson breathed out a sigh of relief, since if they weren't sending a whole little mini-armada, it seemed as if they weren't about to be attacked. Yet, something inside him remained on full alert. Why were his mutant senses quivering as if they'd just been hit with a sledge hammer?

The raft pulled up to the shore and Rockson could see just below the surface of the mist hundreds of the writhing five-foot snakes were accompanying the craft. Rockson was glad that he wasn't a fulltime poleman in these hellish swamps.

"The one called Rockson," the head poleman shouted out as the Freefighters gathered around the shore, looking on curiously. The rafters had cold, unfriendly faces, a fact which Rockson didn't like at all.

"Yeah, I'm Rockson," the Doomsday Warrior replied. "What is—"

"Quiet," the raftsman replied, with a most chilling tone. "Pick your top four men and come with us. The king wishes to speak with you once more. Now!"

"Chen, Detroit, Archer, Sheransky, grab a few Lib's—nothing too bulky," the Doomsday Warrior said, using the slang word for their weaponry as the guards wouldn't notice. The king had allowed them to keep their firepower and all their equipment.

"What the hell?" McCaughlin blurted out, not a little anger in his voice. "I've been with the team longer than that Russian there," he said, glancing over at the defector. "Longer than the mountain man even," he

96

added, giving Archer a glance of disdain. "Why can't I come?"

"Come on, pal," Rockson said, hiding the exasperation in his voice. For grown men, his elite team could fight and feud like teenagers from time to time. "I need to keep someone in charge behind—just in case," Rock went on, checking his shotpistol and slamming it into his hip holster. "If something should happen, I need someone to keep an eye on the rest of the crew. They'd be like chopped liver out there in the wilds without some son-of-a-bitch knowing what the hell he's doing. You got me?"

McCaughlin mumbled a few choice things under his breath. "Well, I guess you've got a point," the big Scotsman finally replied, folding his arms across his chest. "But nothing's going to happen to you anyway. We'll be ready to split the moment you get back."

"Thanks, big man," Rockson said, slapping the Freefighter on the shoulder. "Let's go," Rockson said, as his four men got onto the raft with him and the raftsmen began poling away. They all shuddered as it looked as if they were poling through a lake of just serpents. Rockson swore he'd never get used to this place or its inhabitants if he ended up living here a hundred years.

It took them only several minutes to reach the king's mini-island and the large pagodalike structure set in the middle of it. There was the smell of several meat dishes being cooked. When they disembarked from the raft, and were led to one of the large outer rooms of the "royal castle," Rock could see now what was happening. Breakfast.

"Ah, my favored guests are here," King Bailey said as he ate from bowls of food on a large wooden table in front of him. "Pull up, please—and help me eat this overly large amount of hearty breakfast."

"What is it?" Sheransky asked, as he seated himself.

"My favorite," the king replied as he stuffed his mouth. "Fried snake-sausage, lizard eggs, and a vine-pudding. Come on now, it tastes as good as it looks."

The Freefighters looked at each other, and then sat down around the table. Not one reached for the food.

"Actually," Rockson said, coughing and glancing around to see just how many guards there were, almost in an unconscious fashion, "We hoped to discuss our leaving. You've been most kind—but we do have to move on. Our hometown is waiting for survival supplies—and we're the suckers out here trying to get it."

"How heroic," the king said, polishing off the last of his breakfast. "And how truly inspiring to see men show such loyalty toward their community." He wiped his mouth with a leaf napkin and motioned impatiently for the bowls and plates to be taken away. Two servants came rushing over and removed the leftovers in a flash. "Yes, of course you can make your exit today—by lunch, if you wish. I'll have my men prepare some food to take with you."

"Thank you. That is generous of you," Rockson said as he let out a sigh of relief. The rest of the Freefighters as well relaxed, as you just never knew what was going to happen next.

"There is just one thing," King Bailey added, licking his fingers.

"And that is?" Rockson asked.

"Oh, we have a little ritual for all those who pass through our lovely kingdom," King Bailey went on. "Just a kind of purification process—so you don't get left with our swamp energy—and we don't have any of your outsider vibrations left with us." He smiled benignly at them, and now Rock's mutant sixth sense was buzzing inside him.

The king rose up from his breakfast nook and motioned around with his head. Nearly a dozen guards, each carrying the long spear probes, rose up as well and surrounded Rock and the rest. On all sides. "Come now, this will be most amusing—for all of us."

Rockson looked around desperately, seeing if there was some escape. But the way they were surrounded, with all those hissing snakes dripping from everyone's shoulders, he knew he had to bide his time until there was an opening.

They were led outside and over to the swamp, and once again loaded up onto one of the larger rafts, the king standing in the front, eyes focused ahead. His aides gave him a cloak covered with several highly colorful banded snakes, which slithered around his shoulders and neck.

They were poled to the north for a good five minutes, a long distance for the town which extended only a few hundred yards itself. The morning was alive with bird-caws and the howling of monkeys in the trees above. A regular cacophony of singing swamp-creatures.

At last they reached another island, this one larger and more barren than any they'd passed so far. The raft pulled up and the Freefighters were marched off the thing. They walked about a hundred feet and Rockson could see by the indentations in the hard dirt that something had gone on, recently too, though for the life of him he couldn't figure out just what the hell it was.

The king seated himself on a log as the guards formed a line on each side. And several stood directly in front, so there would be no attempts of the Freefighters charging any of them.

"I must put on the circuses to amuse my people," King Bailey said, folding his arms and leaning back. "Now, I would like a little entertainment for myself, a little circus just for me. And if you do well—then you may leave. You and all your men, just as I've promised."

"Well, bring out the juggling balls," Rockson said with a failing grin. "Not that any of us know how to juggle."

"Oh, but of course," the king responded with a dark laugh. Rock's mutant senses were on overdrive now. Somehow he knew it wasn't juggling that they were about to face. Four of the guards, each holding one of the big horn gourds, blew hard on them. Then again. The sounds exploded in the air, sending the monkeys and other swamplife scurrying off around the north end of the football-field-sized island.

Suddenly, there was a deep furrowing in the swamp waters about a hundred feet out. And Rockson saw what it was that the monkeys and owls and God-knew-what were fleeing for their lives from: a huge head emerged from the black swamp surface as the horns kept blowing. A snake head that must have been the size of ten men emerged from the wetness and started up onto the island. The Doomsday Warrior's throat suddenly constricted and his lips and tongue went dry. Suddenly he was jealous of the little, squealing monkeys high in the trees.

Chapter Twelve

Rock and his team all backed slowly away, keeping several feet apart as the immense serpent emerged dripping from the swamp. The snakemen kept blowing on their gourds, producing a most unearthly sound. It clearly kept the big brute under some sort of control. The black-and-brown-and-red-banded monster had scales the size of shields and a hideous, misshapen face. The way it flicked its tongue didn't make any of the Freefighters all that cheered up either, as it wriggled out of the black swamp surface. It lifted its immense head up a good twenty feet off the island ground. It turned its great pumpkin-eyed face from side to side like some kind of nightmarish radar dome. It was clearly checking things out, in spite of its tremendous power.

"I don't think I've ever seen anything so ugly—" Detroit gulped as the Freefighters backed slowly away from the immense slithering beast.

"He looks pretty damn hungry," Sheransky said, his Adam's apple bobbing up and down.

"Son-of-a-bitch looks like he could eat the whole island," Chen muttered, feeling under the sleeve of his black ninja suit for the dozen starknives.

"No, I think he wants us for appetizer," Sheransky added, his face pale as white flour. It was one thing to fight men, but a whole different story to be staring into the hellish face of a gigantic monster.

"He's a magnificent specimen, isn't he?" King Bailey laughed as he clapped his hands together like an excited child. "We call him 'No,'—because no one or no thing ever gets away. He was much harder to learn to control than most of our other swamplife here. But it's all a question of melody—and once my trumpet-gourd blowers got it figured out—well, it's all pretty simple, really. And he hasn't had any humans to munch on for over a year. We don't get that many visitors these days," King Bailey went on, taking out some dried swamp grass and pressing it down into his makeshift carved pipe.

"You bastard—you set us up! All your hospitality, everything—just a load of bull," Detroit said angrily, wishing he had more than two grenades—a whole lot more.

"Oh no, that was all real," the king smirked. "We are hospitable. We just didn't tell you the final outcome. There's no dishonesty there."

"And if we kill the thing," Rockson interjected as he motioned for the men to spread out as the thing suddenly caught their hot human scent, and started slithering slowly toward them from about a hundred feet off. "We get to leave—all my men, 'brids, everything?"

"If you kill it?" King Bailey laughed as the snakemen

104

around him, holding their long spear-prongs, joined in, as if that was just about the most humorous thing they had ever heard. "Yes, of course, of course," the king grinned, waving his hand like, "let's get on with it." "If you kill it, you can go. You and all your men. I swear that by the great Barnum himself!"

He clapped his hands several times and the horn blowers changed their tune, apparently signaling that it was okay for the mutant snake to strike. And he got the message. The creature made a long, hissing sound like air being let out of a tire a football-field long. Then its eyes quickly scanned the Freefighters. It apparently didn't relate to King Bailey—or his guards.

"Circle him, break up and keep weaving," Rockson yelled out at the elite team, "so he can't take any of us with one bite. Any ideas you have—spit them out. I've got to be honest with you—I don't have the slightest inkling of how to take on this overweight worm. Chen, you have some starknives hidden away?" The guards had stripped them of their shotpistol weapons as they came onto the island. Rock could see his pearl-handled shotpistol lying on the grass near the king. But with all the guards, the weapon might as well have been a thousand miles away.

"I do, Rock," the Chinese-American martial arts master shouted back over the sounds of the gourd horns, which the snakemen kept playing apparently just to let the snake know whose side it was on. "I'm waiting to see how it moves at its most vulnerable points."

"I've got two grenades, Rock," Detroit bellowed out. "Like the karate man himself said—waiting to see what's up! Those scales look as thick as King Arthur's

105

shield. Don't want to waste what we don't have."

Archer let out a bellowing sound that sounded something like "KIIIILLL!" and ripped a two-foot-long, Bowie-type blade from his leg holster, holding it up and waving it around like a steel baton. Rock took out his own flesh-slicer, smaller than the mountain man's, but just as deadly. Sheransky slid an expanding steel rod he had been carrying sewn into the seam of his fatigues. Only twelve inches long, it expanded lengthwise when a button was pressed, to over a yard. Very effective against humans, since it could break a bone with a single strike.

The snake suddenly seemed to choose Archer, perhaps because he was the biggest of them, and caught his eye. Just like a fat man reaching for the huge slice of custard pie first, before turning to his vegetables. Archer's macho indifference suddenly turned to real fear as the snake opened up in full undulation and came rapidly with a sideways kind of motion at the near-mute.

"Move, baby, move," Rockson screamed out from his position about a hundred feet to the left.

"Zig-zag!" Detroit screamed out to Archer, who was already moving. There's something about a creature you could live inside coming after you, with a tongue the size of a water main flapping in and out, and fangs like threshing-blades ready to take you down. Though the mountain man had wrestled down a few bears in his day—he couldn't quite see where he would get a headlock on this son-of-a-bitch!

"Everyone!" Detroit yelled out as the snake passed by him about forty feet off, hot in pursuit of the mountain man, "Stay back." He shouted to Rockson and Sheransky, who were on his side of the thing, "I'm going to try a grenade." He pulled back his right arm and let loose with a speedball pitch that tore toward the thing's side. They all threw themselves to the ground as it hit. It exploded with a muffled roar and a little cloud of smoke.

But then they looked up; it hadn't done a lot of damage, to say the least. A few of the gargantuan scales had been torn loose for a yard or so. But there were just more of the same scales underneath. The thing was built in layers composed of half-inch-thick leathery scales in rows set atop one another. They were going to need an H-bomb—or two.

But at least it brought Archer enough time to get another sixty or seventy feet ahead, as the snake turned to see what all the noise was about. It slowed down only for a second or two, quickly snapping its head back around, searching for the prey that had been so close to its jaws it could taste him. Then it revved up and started forward again.

The problem with being on an island with such an overgrown thing coming after you, Rockson was realizing with great insight, was that there was nowhere to go. Yet they had to do something, or they'd die a horrible death.

"Down, everyone," Chen screamed, while the snake was just getting itself going again. They dropped without questioning the command and the Chinese master let loose with two shuriken from about eight feet off, right into the belly of the "No" creature. They spun through the air with a whistling sound and found their target. The plastique that was mixed right into the six-pointed blades went off with powerful snaps of mini-thunder, and they all looked on hopefully.

More scales had been blown off, and a small stream of greenish-hued blood oozed out from a foot-wide wound. But this time the snake didn't even bother to stop and check it out.

"We're in trouble," Rockson said, as his brain frantically searched for some solution to this mess. But there was nowhere to go except into the swamps, where he was sure they'd meet up with something equally murderous, if not quite as big. The Doomsday Warrior knew they'd have to deal with "No," here and now.

"Both of you," Rock shouted out to Chen and Detroit. "We'll have to try a frontal. A few grenades, some shuriken—maybe we can do some damage up there, take out an eye, rip its head off—anything."

They ran alongside the thing, staying about sixty feet off in case the snake suddenly made a sharp turn. "Archer," Rock yelled out as the big man turned his head, trying not to slow down even an inch. The snake was slowly catching up again, now about a hundred feet from its quarry. "We're coming with more boom-boom," Rock screamed. "When I shout 'Down!' hit the dirt. Got it?"

"MEEEEE GOOOTT!" the near-mute howled back, not needing a hell of a lot of persuasion on any score that held out the slightest chance of rescue. Rock, Chen, and Detroit tore as fast as their legs could carry them and managed to come up alongside the creature as it was closing in on Archer.

"Now!" Rockson shouted out. The big man came flying to the side in a mighty dive. Chen and Detroit pulled back their arms and let loose with a grenade and two shuriken as the snake slowed and scanned to its

108

right to see what was going on. The two pieces of explosive ripped through the dank air and both went off in the thing's face.

As the smoke cleared, they could see a big gash below its right eye, and another smaller one on the side of its mouth. But if anything, they had just made it angry—not wounded or particularly slowed down. It raised its huge head and let out with a howl that sounded like a whole pack of wolves, perhaps an elephant or two, letting out with love-calls.

"Shit on a stick," Rock said as they quickly pulled Archer from the ground and the men looked at each other with confusion and the realization that they were all going to die within minutes at most. "What's left to hit it with?" Rock asked the others. Sheransky held up his steel stick, which looked pitiful to do anything against the monster.

"I'm out," Detroit replied, looking depressed.

"I've got four shuriken left," Chen said in a calm, neutral tone. "But they haven't done anything, as you've seen, except maybe give it a good cleaning on some of its outer scales."

"Then maybe we shouldn't use them directly," Rock said, with a sudden brainstorm which filled his mind with clarity. "Hey, see that small tree over there?" he pointed toward a four-inch-thick, perhaps twelve-foot-high, black-barked tree about seventy feet ahead of them. "Chen, send out a few of your star blades—down near the base. Remember the Cyclops story? Well, we're about to add a few details."

"We'd better move if we're going to do much of anything," Detroit whispered, "because our overblown friend is on his way. And he ain't looking for the 8:05 to

Baltimore." They tore away from the thing again as Rockson heard King Bailey clapping and making various comments to his guards. Apparently he thought this was more fun than a barrel of circus monkeys. They moved hard and fast and came to about twenty feet from the tree, puffing from the exertion now.

"Do it," Rockson ordered as he motioned for the others to drop down. Chen released two more explosive shuriken. There were two more puffs of mini-thunder and, when the smoke cleared almost instantly, they could see that the starknives had nearly blown the whole bottom out of the tree. Nevertheless, it was still standing shakily. They rushed over, as the snake came barreling toward them, and the five Freefighters grabbed hold of the tree. They pushed, but the tree didn't move. But Archer, without a word, just ripped out his oversized blade and with two sharp slashes, the tree was felled.

"Keep it low," Rock shouted to them, as they grabbed hold. "Hold it low, so that hell worm doesn't know what we have in mind—until it's too late."

"Got you, Rock!" they replied, and got a firm grip as they started forward like knights in a joust against some mythical death creature.

"Aim for the head—the eyes if we can. Once it's blinded, it's ours, the biggest link of breakfast sausage ever seen on the planet Earth!" They started rushing toward the thing as it came right at them with a look of confusion on its snake-face. It couldn't remember any creature coming toward it in all its murderous days. But that was fine. The creature opened its mouth in anticipation.

Suddenly it was upon them, and Rockson screamed out for the men all to drive it in past the fangs dripping saliva and poison. The Freefighters peered into that voluminous mouth and throat and sheer fear gave them extra strength. The tree-spear slid right up inside past the tongue and glanced up at a sharp angle, as it hit something hard inside. In a flash the tip of the black tree came tearing out of the top of the skull, as brain and all kinds of green muck came exploding out with it.

The Freefighters all dove to the side, as the head was only feet away from them. But the writhing, slime-dripping nightmare with green blood all over its face didn't seem to care too much about lunch anymore. It was too busy feeling an agony it had never experienced. It went rolling off to the side, over and over, spraying out all that had been inside its skull as the tree-spear, imbedded to about eight feet, just kept digging deeper.

It rolled a good hundred feet, flipping over and over like a worm caught on a fishing hook, the massive body snapping around so Chen and Detroit, who were nearest to it had to jump away, covering their heads. But it just missed, as it snapped spasmodically over-head. Then suddenly, it stopped. The whole body quivered but the head lay still.

Chapter Thirteen

Rockson turned toward King Bailey with a look of triumph on his strong face. "We carried out our end of the bargain!" The Doomsday Warrior snarled out more: "So now if you would—I and my men have a long way to go. And it would be good if we got an early start on the day."

The king looked somewhat amazed at the defeat of his huge pet, even as it lay still a hundred yards off. And he looked angry, very angry, his face quivering with rage. For the immense snake had not just been used for the king's sport—and for disposing of those he didn't want around—but it had also been the symbol of his power. "No" had added a certain fear in the other, lesser snakemen's psyches. But you sure as hell weren't going to be afraid of a pile of rotting scales. He could see that his very power base had been threatened. He could see, as well, that he'd have to be very careful with these Freefighter bastards. They were far more clever and resourceful than he had imagined.

"Yes, yes, of course you can all go now. I can't say I

enjoyed your defeat over the great serpent—but a deal is a deal. We'll just head back to the village—and whatever you need—just tell me—and it's yours." The other snakemen looked at each other as the Freefighters loaded back up onto the raft. They had never seen the king so forgiving, so seemingly unconcerned about what was clearly a major defeat for his authority. As they were poled back on the large raft, Rockson saw the king whispering to several of his top lieutenants at the foot of the craft. Several times he looked around and Rock could sense beneath the false smile a look of incredible hate, as if he wished he could rip Rockson and his pals to shreds on the spot.

His own team felt it too. The king looked as if he was going to explode from barely repressed rage at any moment. Rockson leaned over to Archer, who stood looking around at the swamplands as if searching for some fruit, something good to eat. He put his arm around the huge Freefighter's shoulder and gave Archer a big smile, as if he wanted to borrow the giant's gems or something. "Listen, pal, I'm going to talk real soft, so no one hears us—but when we get back to the island and we all start getting off—I want you to grab the Snake-King there."

"GRRAAAB SNAAAKE MAAAN!" the immense Freefighter replied, trying to whisper, which was a little difficult for Archer. He looked at Rockson thoughtfully as the words sank in. Archer gave Rock a quick nod, his eyes lighting up with comprehension.

"Yeah," Rock went on, "sure is a damn hot and sticky day," so King Bailey wouldn't get suspicious. Chen, Detroit, and Sheransky stood around the back of the pole-driven raft, keeping a sharp eye out for any

114

other demonic creatures that might pop out of nowhere. They had taken out the snake, but that didn't mean diddly about the next thing that might pay them a visit. The Doomsday Warrior continued whispering to Archer: "When I give the 'go' signal, I want you to get that bastard in a nice headlock."

"HEEADLOOCCK," the near-mute echoed back, glancing up at the front of the raft as if checking out the king's neck and head for a fitting.

"Don't kill him—but if the shit hits the fan—rip his goddamned head from his body. Understand?"

"UUUNNDEEERRSSTAAANNNDD!" Archer said, with a big grin stretching across his face. He knew he had been given a very important assignment, a responsibility that he didn't often get. Besides, it would be fun to take the king out, after what he had just put them all through.

"Good man," Rockson said with a grin, slapping the grizzly bear-sized Freefighter on the back. It was like slapping the side of a tree, and he grimaced slightly as he pulled his hand away. He glanced back at the rest of the team and gave two handsignals invisible to any of the snakemen but clear enough to his own crew: "Something is up—be prepared but don't make a move."

They acknowledged.

After about five minutes, they reached the king's palace of trees and vines. The raft came sliding up to the wide terrace that surrounded it. As he got off and jumped up a foot to the wooden platform, Rock and Archer came tearing after the bastard. King Bailey turned back with sudden fear on his face as he saw the two Freefighters barreling down on him. Before any of

115

his men could swing their death-poles on them, Archer was alongside the king and threw both his arms into some kind of mountain-style wrestling hold around his royal neck. It looked as if he could snap the man's neck like a chicken bone.

Three of the personal guards started forward fast, but Archer tightened the grip even further and half-lifted King Bailey right off the platform. The man gurgled and sputtered, waving his hands like a madman.

"No, stay back," the king managed to spit out. The guards stopped, as they suddenly saw that the Freefighter could kill their ruler in about half a second if he pulled just a little harder.

"Okay, Bailey," Rockson smirked as he walked up to the snake emperor and made a slow circle around him. Everyone else froze as they watched. "You want to live, I'm sure. But since my friend here could crush your larynx into pulp, I'd advise you to do what I say. Got it?"

"Yes, yes, I hear you," King Bailey replied, his face turning red. "Whatever you want, I promise."

"Good," Rockson said, slapping the snakeman on the arm as if they were the best of friends. "Loosen it up, Archer; so you don't accidentally rip something off," the Doomsday Warrior said. The near-mute loosened the wrestling grip just a notch or two. King Bailey came down onto his feet again and the lobster red coloration of his cheeks and face dropped to a slightly pinker color.

"First," Rock said as he motioned for his team to gather round, "we want all the weaponry your guards took from us when we landed here yesterday. Load them up onto the raft." He nodded toward his team to follow.

"Yes, yes, they're all in the storage chamber in my palace." He ordered five of his inner elite bodyguards to go in and bring it all out. Within minutes, the snakemen, along with Rock's own men were carrying armfuls of rifles and supplies back out to the raft. It felt good to have their full array of armaments. Detroit grabbed his twin bandoliers of grenades and slipped them around his chest. His face broke into a broad smile. There was something about being fully armed and ready to kick booty that made things a little brighter.

"Okay, let's move," Rockson shouted out to them all when he saw they were loaded up. "Now, this is the story," the Doomsday Warrior spoke to King Bailey, as Archer dragged the man back onto the raft. "We're going to head to the island where the rest of my men and our 'brids are. I want you to get the two other rafts that brought us to this foul-smelling swamp. Then you're going to lead us out of here, since we don't know these wandering mud-pathways. No one tries to stop us, no one plays around. Do you understand what I'm saying?"

"Yes, yes," King Bailey said, with coughing desperation. "Two more rafts," he croaked out to a good dozen of his men standing on the platform.

Within minutes the rafts were alongside them with their pole-crews. They poled off away from the snake temple and toward the prison-island as hundreds of the snake people stared in amazement at the sight of their king being held prisoner. But none made a move as he kept gurgling for them to keep back. Archer had a goofy grin on his face as they poled along. He was the center of attention, and he loved it.

The rafts pulled up to the island where Rockson was overjoyed to see that his men were unharmed. They were pretty happy to see him too. The idea of losing their commander was, to say the least, not their favorite daydream. Aside from liking Rock, they all knew that they didn't have a snowball in hell's chance of getting out of this place alive without his ability and judgments all the way. McCaughlin would *try* hard, but this was a job for the Doomsday Warrior!

"Load up," Rock shouted out, as the rafts pulled up onto the shoreline. Instantly the men rushed and got the hybrids which were tethered to some ropes about two hundred feet off. They carefully led the mutant horses up onto the rafts and then got their equipment packed onto their mounts. One of the 'brids slipped as it was getting aboard and floundered around in the black surface waters as some snakes came streaming through the current. But one of the gourd men let out a sharp sound and the snakes veered off at the last second. The 'brid was dragged back up to shore and then led, whinnying and dripping, onto the raft. The other mounts grew nervous but at least they were more careful, staying as much as they could toward the center of the rafts.

"Everyone and everything aboard?" the Doomsday Warrior shouted out as he surveyed the chaos of men and animals.

"You got it, Rock," McCaughlin yelled back, as they made a quick head count.

"Move them doggies out," Detroit laughed, glad to be getting out of the dank hellhole.

"Okay, Chiefie," Rockson said, walking over to Bailey. "Let's get this real straight. I don't want problems, any accidents, any *anything*. Take us north until we reach solid land. I've got a compass, so don't try any tricks either. Otherwise you ain't going to have a neck!" Archer tightened up a little, just to remind the man of his present situation.

"Absolutely—no problems," the Snakeman King gulped hard. "I'm no fool." He addressed his polers, and the gourd man on each raft blew his signals to keep their snake-army off. The rafts began poling past the village, slowly at first, but as they built up some momentum, the craft hit a half-decent "cruising" speed. Snakes slithered near them in the swamp but didn't approach, as the gourd men let out little toots on their instruments. The Freefighters began relaxing more and more as they drew away from the village and the snakes.

Alongside them in high trees they could hear and see monkeys dancing around, making a noisy spectacle of themselves. Huge python-like serpents hung down from wide branches, but didn't come any closer.

Here and there, the men could see shapes splashing from the shorelines of the hundreds of little islands that they passed. At first Rockson thought they were snakes as well, but on closer inspection he could see they were alligators. The gourd sounds didn't seem to affect them one way or another. But being poked by the long pole prongs kept them at bay. Though they shadowed the rafts, hoping something or someone would fall off, the alligators didn't make any aggressive moves. A monkey, one that had gotten too near the end of its branch, lost its balance and tumbled down into the swamp water. In a flash two of the 'gators ripped the hapless mammal into two bleeding pieces. They swallowed hard and the animal was gone, as if it had never existed.

They poled on for almost an hour as the swamp widened more and the water grew a little clearer. At last Rock could see the low mountains that surrounded the valley swamp just ahead, looming out of the mists.

"This is it," King Bailey groaned again as Archer let his arms relax slightly so the prisoner could talk. "That bank there."

"Have your men pole us over to that shore," Rock said as he scanned the solid ground just ahead of them. King Bailey shouted out commands to his crew and the rafts were quickly poled up onto the bank of black mud which grew solid after a few feet. Rock had his whole team drag their 'brids from the rafts onto shore. He had the polers throw their equipment into the swamp, so they couldn't suddenly try to attack them, and then had his men all mount up. "But," complained the king, "you can't leave us without our pole-weapons!"

"Sure I can," Rockson said, with a cynical expression as he looked at Bailey. "I can see the valley wall right ahead. Your men can dive for the damned poles. But you look sweaty from this little trip in the country. Archer, maybe our friend here needs a little bath to get the grime off?" He nodded his head twice, as all the blood drained from the king's face.

"No, no! Please! Not the swamp! Not the—" But Archer was already lifting the man high over his head, and with a slight bend in his massive legs the Freefighter threw him as far as he could into the swamp.

Bailey splashed around in the water feet first, but before his guards could swim out and extricate him, several immense heads rose from the water. And even as the snakemen looked on in horror, the alligators charged at their king. Several of them snapped their massive jaws around the snakeman's extremities. And with hundreds of red bubbles foaming and a final scream, Bailey was pulled down into the swamp.

And didn't surface again.

Chapter Fourteen

They rode for ten hours, and camped in a nice, dry spot. The first thing Ted Rockson saw when he awoke the next morning was a large, black, ugly bird, with wings that must have been at least eight feet across and a strange hooked beak. It was flying in circles perhaps ninety feet above him, its red eyes looking down with great curiosity.

Suddenly it swooped lower, the table-sized wings flapping out sharp snapping noises in the air. Rock's heart sped to double time as he reached for his shotpistol. But the moment he had the gun in hand and his arm thrust out, the great bird saw the motion and was already swooping away, the huge black wings releasing a few feathers here and there as they stroked hard. The bird gave him a quick little turn of the head as it tore across the prairie, and then was just a dot in the sky.

Rock had almost fired before he realized what it was—a vulture. A big one, but vultures are only interested in the dead. These huge birds were carrion eaters. He had never seen one go after something living, not even a rabbit or small mammal. It was just one of nature's scavengers, a living vacuum cleaner without which the environment would be filled with the rotting flesh of tens of thousands of animals.

He looked around with a sheepish expression on his face, but no one had seen the action. Next he'd be firing at chameleons and ants, at the rate he was going.

The rest of the men were just starting to rise up themselves, yawning and stretching out their arms. Rockson sat up and slipped the big .12-gauge shotpistol back into its home and jumped to his feet.

"Rise and shine," an annoying voice shouted out as he banged a coffeepot against some other loud cooking utensil. The Scotsman walked around the encampment, slamming two music makers together as if he were trying to wake the dead. "Up, up, before you miss one of my amazingly tasty wasteland breakfasts," McCaughlin bellowed. "With real eggs. You hear me—real eggs." Men groaned and a number of not very savory phrases came hurtling back at him.

"Come on now, men," the Scotsman said with mock hurt. "I've been up since dawn—found some eggs. Cooked up a whole shitload of snake-sausage too. You'll all be happy if you come get some chow. Before it runs out." He banged the pots a final brain-jarring time and headed back to his fire.

None of them was particularly enthusiastic about either getting up or eating snakes. But since the only culinary alternative was the energy packets in the 'brid bags, they made themselves move over to the fire. Even Rockson stumbled over, feeling unusually sleepy this morning. The food he forced down without much enthusiasm, even though he knew it was pleasing his stomach a lot better than Shecter's synth-chow. It was the coffee, even if it was hydroponically grown, that got his juices going.

While the others finished up, Rock took out field binocs and surveyed the land ahead from Snorter's back, jumping up onto the animal's broad shoulders and grabbing hold of the hanging mane. He could see herds of bison, other smaller creatures that looked like a cross between a mountain goat and large deer. Rock had never seen a hybrid mix quite like that before. On the other hand, everywhere he went, every terrain seemed to bring new creatures. The old days, the old pre-war animals—were gone forever. God knew what the bison ate out here. It didn't seem as if there was nearly enough to sustain such large herds of big animals. But there must have been something just at the ground's surface, or even hidden below it, to sustain them.

The autocompass on the side of binocs showed him north. He didn't always trust the direction finders, especially since the magnetic pole seemed to keep shifting over the years, sometimes slowly, sometimes changing a number of degrees within hours. Old Shecter explained it with all kinds of complex facts, including axial shift, gravitaton readjustments between the sun and the earth, and so on. Rock never quite understood it all; he wondered if even Schecter did, as the man didn't like to admit he didn't know what was going on in any subject. But between the high-tech binocs, the direction of the sun, and his own mutant sixth sense, Rockson figured it was as good a guess as anything.

"All right, let's load up," the Doomsday Warrior

said, turning and shouting from atop Snorter's back. "You bastards have had your chance to be lazy enough this fine morning.'

As the men gathered their gear together, McCaughlin quickly broke down the mini-kitchen. He seemed able to put up or break down, in just minutes, a full "Cookie" setup!

Just when Rockson was wishing for another cup of the black brew, they were ready to move on. The prairieland was actually fairly hard-packed once they got farther out on it. The sandy ground compressed instantly and the hybrids' hooves hardly sank in at all. Yet, they moved fairly slowly at first as Rockson never trusted anything he didn't know, be it human, animal, or terrain. But it was clear after about five minutes that this stuff was solid enough, and he had them all moved to medium cruising speed. He kept lifting up his binocs every five minutes or so to scan all around them.

The bison herds were right ahead of them. Vast blankets of brown and black. And for a while, as they trotted through the wastelands, Rock wondered whether they should go through the tens of thousands of the slowly moving, grazing creatures or search out some circuitous route. But they had already lost about thirty-six hours; he just couldn't afford to lose any more. The citizenry of Century City were surely going through their own hell. The Freefighters couldn't do any less.

"We're going right through the center of that herd," Rockson addressed the men, turning in his saddle but not slowing perceptibly. "I don't think we should have any problems with them. They're vegetable eaters and

126

slow. They don't even have the right teeth to chew on flesh. But keep your firepower handy. If something charges—take it out."

"You got it, boss," Chen responded as he held up a few starknives, that suddenly just appeared from beneath his sleeve. The man was a proverbial magician when it came to fighting. For the thousandth time Rockson was grateful that the Chinese martial arts master was on their side and not the enemies'.

They rode on for another twenty minutes or so and the vast numbers of bisonlike creatures grew overwhelming. They just spread out across the plains like an army, each one standing nearly as tall as a full-grown hybrid. And yet Rockson knew that even this army was nothing. In the old days, before the Europeans had come into America, there had been herds a million strong that had spread over whole states. Early settlers had described the vast migrations as totally unimaginable unless seen with one's own eyes. This bunch wasn't doing too shabbily now, Rockson noted with a certain satisfaction. The bison had, after all, been left basically alone for over a hundred years.

As he reached the outer edge of the nearest band of bison, Rockson saw what they were eating: a hardly visible coating of a whitish brown weed that virtually covered the prairie, but only for an inch's depth or two. You could hardly see the foodstuff, unless you were just a few feet from it. The grain, or whatever the hell it was, must have been highly nutritious as all these animals were surviving, even growing fat off it.

A few of the great horned mammals looked dully up

as Rock had his team slow down. They blinked a few times with their mug-sized eyes and then dropped their immense heads back down to important things like chewing. But as Rock slowed his team down and led them right through the herd, the buffalo hardly even deigned to look up. In the animal world, only quick motions caused reactions. Predatory movements, things coming in fast. That would sure as hell set this bunch going.

"No fast movements," Rock shouted out to the team behind him. "These animals aren't going to bother us unless we startle them in some way."

Most of the bison didn't lift their huge heads, being too busy pursuing the next little pieces of grain and the stalks beneath them. And as they moved slowly along, the bison let out big loads of steaming fecal waste.

"Rock, do you notice something funny about the sky ahead?" Chen asked as he rode up alongside the Doomsday Warrior. "Almost straight north," the Chinese-American Freefighter pointed, holding his combat binoculars in his hand as they moved at slow gait through the blanket of bison.

"Yeah, I see what you mean," Rock said as he stared through his own binocs. He got a worried look on his face. The northern horizon was getting dark, very dark. Even as he watched, it was as if someone were pulling a set of curtains as thick as iron over the whole stretch of sky. "It looks like a cloudburst—only it's too dark," the Doomsday Warrior added nervously. "And it's coming fast."

"I hate to say what I think it is," Chen said as he scanned the area again with his glasses. "A dust storm—and it's coming like a freight train." He looked around him and saw that the buffalo were starting to look up at the sky themselves, getting their own anxious reactions. There were bleating sounds everywhere, as the herd began picking up speed, heading due east. Animals didn't need mechanical devices to know what the hell was going on around them. And this bunch knew they were about to be blasted with gritty sand, coming in hard and fast.

Rock looked at the fast-approaching darkness. The swirling cloud of sand was coming right at them, with minutes at most to escape it. He scanned his binocs the other way, searching for the slightest bit of cover. About a half mile to the left, he saw a large mound of something. Shelter of some sort, a windbreak at least.

"Come on, men!" the Doomsday Warrior yelled out over the increasingly hard-driven hooves of the bison, which headed by them on all sides. "We got a dust storm moving in," Rock went on. "Our only chance is to make that mound of junk over there."

They tore in that direction as the cloud came shooting in. Now it was a roar like a hundred freight trains on the rails of hell, all racing straight at them. Suddenly it was upon them, and in a flash Rock couldn't see or hear the others.

"Chen, Detroit—anyone there," he shouted above the winds as he had to half-shut his eyes to avoid being blinded by the hurricane force dirt-particles. Someone's voice came shouting back but he couldn't even hear the words. This whole prairie crossing had turned from a snap into a disaster in about the time it took to sneeze.

Rockson cursed himself, as he didn't know what the

hell was going to happen to them now. And suddenly, a gust of sand came in with the power of a Mack truck. It ripped right at him and the 'brid, sending them flying right off the ground. And as if a dream, the Doomsday Warrior was being lifted off the prairie and up into the air where there was no gravity or light. Just sand flying everywhere. And then everything went black.

Chapter Fifteen

It was like being a toy top, just spinning around and around, not knowing where sky began or ended, where the ground itself was. Then suddenly, Rockson slammed with his 'brid into the ground, tumbling for what seemed like hours. He could hear the screaming sandstorm as it whistled by all around and could hear Snorter braying hysterically.

Then they were up again, over the storm-wracked prairie. The Doomsday Warrior couldn't see even a foot in front of him; he felt them both hit ground again, and then roll down a slope like a nonsymmetrical ball. Somehow he hung on to the sturdy 'brid which kept trying to find its balance, to figure out what the hell was going on. Its secondary eyelids surely had shut tightly to protect its eyes. It could see through them, though it was like looking through distorted plastic.

They seemed to turn over dozens of times, rolling down the slope. Rockson had somehow always thought of sand as basically a soft substance. But these grainy bullets, millions of them hitting his face and hands, were more like little pieces of glass. Whenever they made contact with flesh, they tore into him, leaving little hot stings on his body. The sound seemed to grow ever louder, as if a fleet of StratoBombers were landing all around him. For all he knew, Rock could have been fifty feet in the air, sucked up in a tornado.

But suddenly, still gripping the 'brid's thick mane like a jockey coming in just inches ahead of his nearest opponent, they reached the bottom of the long slope and slammed into the prairie. Hard. This time, Rockson went flying off Snorter as if he were a bowling ball that had been released down a sand-covered bowling alley. He hit the ground rolling over and over, keeping his eyes and face shielded from the swirling dust beneath and all around him. At last he came to a completed stop and lay there for a few seconds, trying to get his bearings and making sure nothing had been broken.

He still seemed whole. He sat up, hardly able to withstand the rushing sand-filled wind, and tried to brace himself, looking around for Snorter who he hoped hadn't broken a leg. The 'brid had been with him for years—and he sure as hell didn't want to shoot the son-of-a-bitch. On the other hand, they probably both were going to die out here, killed and dissolved automatically by the sand—so why worry about it? Rockson let out a cynical laugh.

He stood up, crouched up anyway, as he saw that he couldn't take the force of the winds blasting around him. The sand must have been blowing in gusts up to 80 mph, even a 100, a veritable hurricane of dust. He started walking around on deeply crouched knees, like a Sumo wrestler.

Where the hell were the others? Had he led them right into their demise? The entire unit must have been taken down into the sand, buried ten, twenty feet down. "Oh, shut up!" Rockson screamed out to his own brain. "Get a hold of yourself!" he shouted in the wind. And got a sandy tongue.

He heard a sound like an elephant coughing and pulled out his .12-gauge. But as he walked on a few more yards, Rock saw that it was the 'brid, half-buried in a pit of sand. It was nearly flat on its back like some immense turtle that had got turned over and couldn't quite get up again. Ordinarily the 'brid wouldn't have found it all that much trouble. But being hysterical and unable to get good footing on the sand, Snorter just sort of rolled around madly. Rockson reholstered the blaster, and taking the reins, helped pull and guide the hybrid up to its feet again.

Rockson couldn't quite decide whether to stay where he was or move around trying to find the others. After a minute's deliberation he decided to move. It wasn't going to get him anywhere just standing there like a statue in a park being eroded by the dust.

He took Snorter by the reins and trying to use his mutant senses to get his bearings, walked slowly into the sandstorm. He followed a tight circular pattern, slowly expanding it as he went, calling out for his men.

"Freefighters?! Freefighters! Anyone the hell out there?" the Doomsday Warrior shouted with a kind of desperation, knowing as he did so that it was unlikely anyone could hear him above the drone of the sand. But had to try. He'd gone in circles for maybe six or eight minutes when he swore he heard sounds ahead. Men and beasts very close. He closed in on the noises

133

and yelled out for whoever was there.

"Rock? Rockson, is that you?" What sounded like Detroit's bellowing tones broke slightly through the sand symphony. He rushed toward the sound, dragging Snorter through the dunes below their feet. Suddenly there were figures in the gray, dusty mists. Two? Three? It was hard to tell.

"It's Rockson!" the Doomsday Warrior screamed out.

"Oh shit, I thought that was it for you," Detroit said, coming out of the curtains of blinding grit. "Thought we'd have to say some prayers over a plaque back at C.C., assuming we ever got there."

"I'm pretty hard to kill," the Doomsday Warrior said, slapping the black man on his outstretched hand.

"Rock!" Chen echoed up, squeezing Rock's shoulder.

Then Archer came stumbling behind his 'brid with an ear-to-ear smile. If Rockson ever kicked off, he didn't quite know what the mountain man would do. It wasn't something he liked to think about. "RRROOOOCCKSSSSOON!" Archer groaned, like a bull-moose in rutting season. He rushed over the last few yards and slapped the Doomsday Warrior so hard on the back that he almost went flying over onto his face.

"Where are the rest of the men?" Rockson asked, as they came out of the fervor of their little reunion.

"Don't know," Chen replied.

The snapping sand still came at all of them like pellets shot out of a cannon. "We suddenly all got separated somehow," Chen related. "McCaughlin's with them. Sheransky too. Last time I saw them. I hope they're able to stay together as a unit. The recruits won't have a chance by themselves or even broken up into single units. Most of those men haven't camped out on their own on crystal clear nights let alone going through a hell like this."

"True!" Rock spat out the word. He'd really screwed up on this one. He took out his shotpistol in desperation and let loose with a few blasts, straight up into the air. He knew it was absurd and the 'brids all jumped back startled, wondering what the hell one of their riders was doing shooting at sand. They had a vague understanding of the workings of the minds of men—but this was beyond them. The pistol's loud roar couldn't have gone more than ten yards in the mess blowing all around them before it was totally absorbed in the deafening sand-void.

"I think it's getting worse," Detroit noted as he stood on the windward side of the 'brid, which was a hell of a lot better suited to take this kind of weather, its hide being nearly as thick as elephant skin. "I can feel the velocity of the particles picking up," he said, addressing the other three as loudly as possible. Only Archer seemed not to particularly notice or care as he stood there listening to the others. For him, no doubt, it was all some sort of lark down to the beach, and he almost seemed to revel in the massaging particles which flew into him from every direction.

"We've got to find shelter," Chen said. "It's coming in too hard. Look down." They stared down at their feet and saw that in the minutes they'd been talking, nearly six inches of sand had piled up around their boots. Stand around for another five—and they'd be human sand dunes, unable to move an inch. "We'll search for the men as soon as this dragon storm dies down a little, as soon as we can see."

They began walking slowly, pulling the 'brids behind them. It was slow going and as they walked, sinking deep into the sand at each step, the wind definitely was picking up. They could hardly move sometimes as it pushed right into them. Even the 'brids were off-balance half the time. It was clear after another five minutes that they weren't going to be able to keep this up too long. But, to say the least, there was nowhere to get shelter.

"We've got to find someplace to hide!" Rock shouted at them, his face now little streams of pencil-thick blood. "Maybe we'll have to shoot two of the 'brids and—" The Doomsday Warrior hated even saying the words and he swore that Snorter whipped his huge head around and gave him the evil eye.

"SHHEELLLTER!" Archer suddenly bellowed out at the end of the trekking crew.

"Damn right, big fellow," Detroit agreed. "We'd better find some fast or—" He slid his hand across his throat to show what would happen to all of them.

"MEEEE KNOOOOW WHEERRRE!" the huge ex-woodsman exclaimed with his booming voice. "FOLLLLLOOOOW!" Without another word he turned and headed to the left. The other three Freefighters looked hard at one another for a few seconds as if they might be taking their lives into their hands by following the giant.

"Got nothing to lose, that's for damn sure," Rockson said, shrugging his shoulders. The three of them followed, this time staying right behind each other so they wouldn't get lost. Archer walked, standing tall, and with all his weight the battering winds hardly seemed to affect him. He seemed to know exactly where he was heading, as if he'd been out here a thousand times before.

They headed through the storm for perhaps five minutes and suddenly the intensity of the sand and wind seemed to drop dramatically. They could even see one another again. They were apparently being sheltered from the wind by a huge mound of rotting vegetation. Sheltering cacti, Rockson could see, as he came into the space.

"SEEEE!" the mountain man said with deep pride, slamming himself on the chest with force that would have taken out a tree or two.

"Son-of-a-bitch!" Detroit exlaimed with absolute amazement on his grit-impregnated face. It felt great to be able to breathe and they all breathed in and out hard, trying to clear their noses and mouths of the cutting particles. The 'brids made similar movements as well. As Rock looked around he saw that it was indeed a mound of cacti, about ten yards' worth. There must have been a grove of them right in this spot. Somehow they all had died and fallen, but had stayed sort of interwoven together as they crumbled down on top of one another. They were somehow still in one piece, but all brown and hollow, with thorns covering everything. It was a mound a good twenty feet high and it extended maybe thirty feet from side to side. The wind blew hard on each side of them, but most of it wasn't getting to them, probably duning up against the cacti on the far side.

"How the hell could he have known about this?" Detroit asked as he slid to his butt behind the thing and sat there, his 'brid looking at him curiously.

"Maybe he smelled it," Rockson replied, following

suit as his legs suddenly felt tired from the efforts of going through what had felt like quicksand. "He was from the mountains, didn't know a hell of a lot of 'civilization's ways' when I found him," Rockson replied. "So maybe some of his more primitive ways haven't been smashed in by society. Who the hell knows? Sense of smell, sound, a lot of things that we hardly experience—are the ways he relates to the whole world. Who cares?"

"Not I," Detroit laughed, taking some water from his canteen.

The winds and sand roared by them on both sides, but here in the center of the protective covering hardly a particle reached them.

"Nor I," Chen said with a grin, twisting his black mustache. "Mountain man or not, he saved our asses."

As if he had heard and understood their every word, Archer came and stood looming over the three Freefighters, looking down at them as a mother might look at her kids as they played in beach sand. He shook his head slowly from side to side as if to say, "What the hell would these dumb bastards do without me?"

Chapter Sixteen

The sandstorm raged all around the rotten cactus windstop like an army, searching for the Freefighters. But try as it might, though a few particles here and there managed to get in their faces, it was nothing compared to what was happening on either side of them. It was strange actually, since they could see one another now that they were out of the actual storm. But right at the edges of the cacti mound, they couldn't see a thing, other than a roaring curtain of gray and brown.

"Pretty nice setup," Chen said with a bemused expression to the others as the four Freefighters sat side by side at the base of the cactus windbreak. "I wonder, though, if the cacti are edible."

"Yeah," Detroit laughed as he juggled two grenades in the air. The others couldn't stand it when he did that. But the pins were still in. Besides, no one had ever seen him drop one. "We can open a Wasteland Soul-Food Franchise out here."

Rockson grinned as each man wisecracked a line or two, keeping up spirits. But his mind was elsewhere on his missing men. He felt like a general who has taken his men into the thick of battle and then just left them there to survive or die on their own. At least McCaughlin and Sheransky were with them, though. The two were among the toughest of his elite Rock team, and had a lot of experience in combat, and were smart as whips in survival skills.

"They'll make it," Chen spoke up. "If any group of men can—this will. After all, they're not like children," the Chinese martial arts master went on. "They're Freefighters, all are volunteers for this mission. Relax, Rock, it's not going to help any of us, especially you, if you just get all spaced out and stop looking where you're going. Then you'll croak, and whatever chance we have of salvaging this whole operation will be put even deeper in the hole. We all know what the odds are out here."

"I hear you," Rock replied softly.

"But most of all," Detroit said, "there ain't shit we can do about it right now."

"ARRCHHEEER HUUUNGRRYYY," the mountain man exclaimed, sitting down with him. He pointed to his mouth and stomach, and made a strange, ugly face. As if he had saved them all, and he damn well deserved something now. They all chuckled and the mood changed dramatically.

"I think I've got something for ya, big fella," Detroit said, reaching around in one of the pockets of his combat jacket. "Well, what have we here?" He pulled out some synth-crackers and a six-inch-long strip of some salted snake McCaughlin had cooked up that morning. "Just saving it for lunch." He handed it out to

Archer, who grabbed it so hard and fast that the black Freefighter ripped his hand back as if a pit bull were going after it. The giant was not the subtlest of men, and slammed the proffered treasure down into his mouth in two quick bites. Then he looked around for some more, his face dropping into something of a forlorn expression as he saw that was it. He slid back down the cactus wall and sat there with his arms folded across his grizzly-sized chest. He grumbled and mumbled weird grunting noises to himself, casting occasional angry eyes at the others. They all pulled back a few inches.

"We'll wait until this damn storm is over—or nearly—and then try to find the men," Rock mumbled, thinking out loud. "Might as well take a snooze. We're sure as hell not going anywhere right away."

Within twenty minutes, listening to the now almost smooth roar of the sand particles roaring by on both sides of the cactus mound, they were in half-dozes. Except for Rockson. No matter what he did, or any of them said, he kept seeing the rest of the expedition buried up to their necks, screaming as their mouths went under the sand. Then, under the spell of the storm's roar, soothing if you weren't out in it, Rock's head slipped down against his chest.

When he awoke, it was morning. The sand was still blowing but it had dropped to only about a quarter of its previous power. The others were already up. Well, most were sitting up straight with their eyes open, anyway. Chen stood in front of them about six feet off doing his Tai-Chi-Chuan exercises. Slowly lifting one foot then the next, turning in tight little circles. He moved with perfect motion, every movement the same speed as the others, his breath totally united with his body, hands. Though they'd all seen Century City's foremost martial arts instructor practice before, what never ceased to amaze them was the sheer perfection of it.

Rockson stood up, stretched and walked to the edge of the cactus windbreak and peered around the edge, shielding his eyes so they wouldn't take a fistful of dust. It was a lot better. They could definitely move out now.

"Time to split, gang," Rockson said, turning back and quickly doing a few stretches and deep knee bends to get the blood going again. The others slowly stood up, everything cracking, joints creaking as if they were about to pop out of their sockets. There was something about sitting or lying in one place for about fifteen hours that did wonders for the body's suppleness, or rather the lack of it.

"What do you have in mind, Rock?" Chen asked as he stopped his exercise, breathed out and then turned toward the Doomsday Warrior.

"Well, we can only hope for the best and assume that Sheransky and McCaughlin found some kind of shelter too. We'll stay together and head north. Do a slow circumnavigation of this whole area in a northerly direction, since that's the direction we were all heading. Any other ideas?"

The others looked at each other and all shook their heads "no" slowly. "Sounds as good as anything I could come up with," Chen said softly.

"Ditto," Detroit added. Archer just looked around, hoping that a synthburger and a big malted milk might just dig their way up through the sands and jump into his hamhock-sized hands. He was clearly getting into a pretty foul mood, not having eaten for a lot longer than he could remember. They all stayed a few feet away. They loaded up the 'brids who had been standing side by side at the end of the cactus windbreak in a kind of meditative trance for the last twenty-four hours. They came right out of it when the men slapped them on the rumps and seemed anxious to get the hell out of there and out into the real world.

They mounted up on the 'brids now as the sandstorm dropped to just a sprinkling. The hybrids were very cautious at first. But once they saw that things were a hell of a lot better than they'd been before, they relaxed and even grew a little frisky. Rockson took the lead and headed them on by compass-direction. He used the binocs compass, still not trusting the damn thing, but at least knowing it had worked before. They headed in a north-northeasterly direction as the dark curtains above slowly cleared and they could actually see more and more of the world around them. Then Rock took them back around to the west again, making circles maybe a half-mile wide. He didn't want to leave the area until he was sure.

But nothing but sand. After nearly two hours of the searching, Chen thought he saw something several hundred yards to their right. They all went galloping over, their hearts beating fast and almost exploding as they drew close and saw a mound of something covered by the sand. Rock was off his 'brid first and down on the ground. There were definitely shapes under the sand and he dug frantically, not wanting to see what he

143

was about to uncover. The others joined him as well and on their hands and knees they scraped away at the mound.

Suddenly Archer reached something hard, and uncovering another foot of sand, he grabbed hold of a horn. It was one of the bison horns! Almost at the same moment Chen reached the horn of another of the big beasts. They dug for another minute just to make sure, and then stood up, sweating hard.

"Well, it ain't our men," Detroit said. "And they are only dumb animals—but still, it's sad. Must have gotten caught alone, completely lost their way."

"There've got to be at least thirty of them down there. A veritable landfill of bison," Chen said with a kind of awe.

"This is how dinosaurs got trapped," Rockson said with his solemn respect for all living things, even when they were no longer living.

They stared at the five heads they had uncovered, the eyes covered with sand, the big pink tongues sticking out nearly a foot. They must have been asphyxiated when the grains of sand began inexorably to have their way over the poor beasts.

"I pray this isn't how our men went out," Rockson half-whispered, wishing he hadn't even said the words the moment they came out of his mouth. None of them replied. They mounted up again and headed off. By now the storm had completely disappeared, working its way south toward the swamplands they had just had the pleasure of spending a short holiday in. The air suddenly felt much lighter, as if a thunderstorm had just passed. And they took deep breaths as they rode along, the 'brids, all of them, breathing the sweet

144

oxygen in as if it was some kind of cooling mentholated gas.

They rode in a northerly direction, slowly making the turns bigger and bigger until they must have moved a good ten miles in this manner without seeing a hell of a lot other than a few dead animals, the sand sliding out of their open mouths. And Rock, although he hated to admit it, just couldn't see how the rest of the team could have made it. But he quickly banished such thoughts from his mind, gritted his teeth, and pushed Snorter a little harder.

Nothing. They couldn't find a trace of the missing team. Not a print in the still slightly shifting sands, not a piece of supply or one of a man's old socks somehow slipped from his pack. It was like looking for a needle in a haystack in this vast ocean of sand. You could drop a whale or two out here and never find them again.

They must have gone another ten miles, still circling slowly to the east and west as Rock had hunches about the Freefighters' whereabouts, when they came to a sloping stretch of land that ran ahead perhaps four or five miles. And suddenly the Freefighters stopped in their tracks.

Standing there about a mile off, like some monument to the very clouds streaming by above, was a gargantuan structure.

It looked like a stadium; some sort of bulbous, huge, concrete stadium. Rockson knew about stadiums from poring over Century City's archives many times since he had arrived there. And this must have been one of the biggest. It was absolutely gigantic. In the books he'd read, in the photographic representations, one didn't even begin to get the immensity of this son-of-a-

145

bitch. It was ovular-shaped with a plastic top of some kind in blue and orange stripes, now faded considerably by the weather after a century.

You could see the huge interweaving steel struts everywhere, and could understand in a flash basically just how the thing had been built, understand the engineering behind it all. From prairie floor to top of roof, it must have risen a thousand feet.

Deroit whistled as they all stood there looking as if they'd seen a living god. It made a man feel a little small, to say the least. Particularly when none of the Freefighters had been around when these things had dotted the land. There couldn't be a hell of a lot of them left; most centers of civilization had been blasted away by the screaming nukes, dropping all over America. This one must have been made damn well. Every wall appeared whole from where they were standing.

"What do you think?" asked Chen, a tone of awe which Rock had rarely heard caught in his throat, as not a man could tear his eyes away. Archer just kept shaking his head in awe. The man had spent 90 percent of his life in the wilds; his only mental comparison of the shape of the structure was an egg. An immense steel egg, that looked as if it could take cannon shells and come out the winner. But whatever lived inside that egg had to be equally huge, so the mountain man reasoned. And when he saw Rockson slowly slip Snorter into low gear, Archer's rough face took on an expression of sheer horror.

"NOOOOOOOO GGOOOOOOO!" the huge near-mute growled out. The others looked at him, first with surprise as he hadn't spoken for a while, and then with a kind of compassion. The big man, who had stared down just about everything out here, was clearly feeling some emotions he didn't like.

"I don't think he wants to go to that fucker, whatever the hell it is," Detroit said to Rockson.

"Well, that's where we're headed. We got missing men to find."

Chapter Seventeen

As they drew closer, checking out the place a little slowly since they had no idea what to expect, Rockson found himself responding on a more primitive level of fear—like what Archer was apparently still under. He didn't really believe it contained some huge pterodactyl with wingspans of a hundred feet and lots of starving infant primeval birds just waiting for the next meal. But still, there was a sense about the place that he could hardly even put his finger on, but nevertheless sent goosebumps coursing up and down his flesh. It was something to do with just how majestic it was, or with the fact that it was out in the middle of nowhere as if waiting to grab hold of the unwary traveler. And perhaps, more than all that—it was old. Millions of men, women, children had tramped through the massive gates and doors that he could now begin to see as they got within a mile of it. He could almost sense them still, running and screaming to catch the sport teams that had played inside.

They came right up to what appeared to be one of the

main doors, although the large, arched openings seemed to spread around the entire domed stadium. Rock rubbed his eyes. He could see guards, seated in old, rickety chairs. The uniformed old men looked up, with neither great curiosity nor the lack of it. Apparently, they must have had some visitors here at least once in a while. Rock wondered if he was hallucinating.

"Howdy," one of the oldest guards said, standing up from his wicker chair. The four guards looked a little peculiar, to say the least. Their faces and bodies appeared normal enough—but the uniforms were sort of like blue suits with thick broad ties, and wide-brimmed straw hats. It made them all look like hicks from the 1920s era. By their sides were huge shields, but when Rockson looked a little closer he could see that they were actually immense campaign buttons, with faded images of politicians. Slogans appeared on them, around the edges, on the bottom of the shields:

VOTE FOR MICHAELSON.
SPINNER—HE'S OUR MAN.
CRANSTON, HE BELIEVES
IN THE WORKING MAN.

Lying alongside the shields were huge needle-like swords. The needle-swords were clearly weapons, the Freefighters could see, but so far the guards weren't going after them. Still, Rock kept his hand near his shotpistol just in case.

"You've gotten here just in time for the Annual Convening—what delegation are you from?" the blue-blazered man asked with a big smile, tilting his straw hat back.

"Well, the—the—" Rockson stuttered for a few seconds, not knowing what the hell he was supposed to answer. He knew that saying the wrong thing to one of these men might mean a fight. What seemed nonsensical and absurd, Rockson had discovered in the past, could yet be important. The wrong answers could be construed as insults to people's cultures. "Colorado!" he blurted out suddenly, as his mutant senses spoke for him. The Doomsday Warrior also had discovered, years before, when you don't have the slightest idea what to say—tell the truth.

"Ah, Colorado! A fine and illustrious state! It has produced many illustrious delegates," the guard went on, with a broad grin. "Yep, I've seen more than a few of your people come and go over the years—and damn good men, all of them. I'll tell you that." The man seemed to love to talk, and Rockson took advantage of that. "What's your name?" Rock asked.

"Name's Simpkins. Assistant Internal Security, Sub-Secretarial." He grinned like a country boy eating ice cream. "These here," he went on, pointing around at his fellow guards, or whatever the hell they were, "are Sub-Junior-Underassistants. But Handelman is a Facilitator. Everything is broken down into ranks here. It makes life so much easier when everyone knows just who and what they and their functions are. Don't you agree?"

"Oh, no question about that, no question at all! Tell me," the Doomsday Warrior went on slowly, not bringing attention to the fact that he didn't know what the hell was going on. He didn't want any of these straw-hatters to know that. "We were, of course, given

151

a certain amount of information back in Colorado—but what exactly is happening here these days? My information is years old. Can you, er—fill me in?"

"Well, I'll be glad to do that!" As the others looked fairly bored, returning to the chairs, Simpkins spoke pridefully to Rock: "This is the Great Caucus Dome—and we, of course, are the Caucus people. You'll see in a minute when you're given the tour. This here is the Republam Convention. We have delegates from around this whole section of the country. Think we're up to almost three thousand Caucus people, in all. Few stragglers still a'comin'."

"But what exactly do you all do?" Rock went on, trying to act nonchalant. "I mean, what's the function here?"

"Well, you know that it goes back to before the war. Our ancestors were holding an Annual Republam Party convention to pick choices for state political office—you know all that! We had rented this huge dome for two weeks—and then the war. Somehow this immense dome survived the holocaust," Simpkins went on, "though according to our notes and compu-secretarials which survived from back there, a huge radioactive cloud virtually covered the place. Our great-great-grandparents managed to survive, by shutting all the vents and water supply off for a month. And that was enough. And we've been here ever since, carrying out our orders. Which is why we're so popular. You know that."

The man looked suspicious now. "Everyone does his bit!"

"And those bits are?" Rockson asked, a little nervously, knowing that was something he should know, having ridden a thousand miles to get here.

"Rules, votes, caucuses, many important functions," Simpkins went on, with pride, and also the beginnings of a little more than just mild suspicion toward Rockson, who seemed to know very little about what was going on. "Why, today is the beginning of our annual Rules Committee elections. Nearly a hundred posts to fill! I find it one of the more exciting times of the year. You all are privileged to be here right now. And then, next week, is the election of Caucus Captains. It's a busy time of year." The man pulled back on his red suspenders which Rock saw that he had on inside the jacket.

"Sounds thrilling," Rock said, glancing around to make sure his own men weren't drifting off. This Caucus fellow seemed to be a fool in a way, but the Doomsday Warrior could see that within that happy-go-lucky fool's exterior he had a brain that was quite observant. But then, if the man were descended from former politicians, that wasn't too much of a surprise. The one thing that Rockson wasn't even beginning to understand was just what the hell these people did. Vote for whom? Caucus for what? He didn't get into that right now. He could see that Simpkins was getting a little more curious about the Freefighters, and had some questions himself.

"Who's that big old country boy?" Simpkins asked, as he took in Archer, seated on the last hybrid.

Archer was looking up and around at the huge Caucus Dome like a kid's first time in the big city. It was so big and round. And now that he saw that it wasn't about to snap them up like some sort of immense venus flytrap, he wanted to go inside and see just what it was. He'd let Rock handle the rest.

"Oh, a—bodyguard," Rockson hesitated, knowing he didn't want to get into detail about any of them. For Simpkins would quickly see that they had nothing to do with the Caucus people

"And you have a Chinese and a black with you as well. You don't see too many of them around here. Thought most of them had been blown up. Well, don't you worry. We ain't got no problems with that stuff here. In fact, I think we got a few of our own, somewhere around the place."

"That's mighty open of you," the Doomsday Warrior replied with a smile. Chen and Detroit did the same.

"Anyway," Simpkins went on, sliding back down into his chair as if all this standing around was starting to tire him out, "that's it." Rock noticed that the guards were all fat as well as old. Where the hell did they get enough food to feed them? And if there were thousands more inside—? This whole place was becoming more of a mystery every minute.

"Handelman," Simpkins said to the man who was sitting at the chair next to the talkative Caucus officer. "You're a Facilitator 2nd Class. Take this crew inside, show them around a little and get them settled into the Junior Delegates commissary. I assume these fellows are hungry," Simpkins said, patting his wide stomach. "Get 'em some chow."

"Ah, do I have to?" asked Handelman, who had a wide handlebar mustache going all across his plump face. It was almost the plaintive whine of a child. This one didn't seem like an Einstein, Rock could see that instantly. "I was just getting some notes together for the kick-off ceremonies tomorrow afternoon."

"You'll do them later," Simpkins replied, with a certain cool demeanor that clearly showed that you didn't want to go against the man, or have him as an enemy.

"All right, Mr. Rockson." Handelman got up from his seat, and scratching his head beneath his straw hat, led them through the main gate. He walked pretty slowly considering he wanted to get back to his notes. "Better get down from your animals here. There's plenty of side tunnels and light fixtures—and all kinds of stuff in here; they could get—"

"TUNNNNEELL," Archer groaned out as the wide corridor stretched on ahead for what looked like miles.

"What's wrong with him?" the Caucuser asked Rockson.

"Oh, he just has a thing about tunnels. You know how it is. He got stuck in one when a child. Also, he was hit in the head a few years ago and—" Rockson shrugged.

The answer seemed to satisfy Handelman, who led them down the long concrete corridor and then took them to the right. They came into a large square room with hay on the floor and the smell of manure thick in the air. There were stables all over the place, maybe a hundred of them with all kinds of breeds eating hay, drinking from buckets of water.

"Here you go, fellows," Handelman said, leading them to the far end where a bunch of stalls were empty. The place looked clean, well cared-for. The smell of horse dung was almost painfully strong toward the back. The other steeds all looked up as the four new hybrids were led in. They hardly noticed, being more

155

interested in their food. Like all living creatures, intellectual curiosity came second to stomach-growl quenchings.

"Stableboy!" Handelman exclaimed, clapping his hands with loud, smacking sounds so that Archer looked over, startled, reaching for his chair-sized crossbow behind his shoulder. A youth in his mid-teens jumped down a storage loft with a magazine in his hands. The magazine was all faded and yellowed, Rock noted.

"Yes, sir," the stable lad said as his eyes quickly rested on the Freefighters' mounts. He whistled as he walked over and patted Snorter on the nose. Rock's 'brid usually didn't like strangers a hell of a lot, especially those who touched it when it didn't necessarily feel like being touched. But the mutant horse didn't seem to mind at all with this kid, and nuzzled his face.

"You're pretty good with these fellows," Rockson commented, smiling at the youth.

"Been around them my whole life," the lad went on as he took Rock's and then Chen's mounts and led them into the open stalls.

"Now, give them some prime oats today," Handelman said, almost scolding the lad although he hadn't done anything wrong.

"What about our supplies that we have all battened down on our animals?" Rockson asked as he patted Snorter on the wide rump as the animal passed by and looked around at its stall a little edgily, making some low whinnying sounds to show its nervous displeasure.

"Easy, boy, you and me going to be good pals," the stableboy said softly in the animal's ear, rubbing his

156

hand down the side of its face. The 'brid quieted down instantly.

"We'll send some porters down here to get it all, once you're settled in," Handelman replied.

Rockson didn't mention their weapons. He wasn't in the mood to give them up. They had only been in the place a few minutes, but already the Doomsday Warrior was feeling a sense of foreboding. There was a strange aura to the place.

"I'll take care of 'em all," the bucktoothed youth said, taking Archer's and Detroit's animals as well and leading them to the next two stalls. Archer gave him a suspicious look, until the kid grinned back innocently. The huge Freefighter relaxed with that and he smiled back his own innocent look. The giant functioned at a fairly primitive level, but he could tell who was okay and who wasn't. The kid was all right. "TAAAKKEEE CAARRRE HORRSIE," Archer said, looking sternly at the lad.

"Don't worry about that!" the stableboy exclaimed. "I love 'brids of all kinds. These are all beauties!" He looked around at the other steeds eating away like threshing machines in the private stalls and then turned toward Rockson, whispering conspiratorially with his hand over his mouth. "Most of these other hybrids ain't the best," the stableboy went on. "They're overweight, ain't been ridden enough, energy level is low. Why even their teeth is bad in a lot of 'em. Sort of like some of the people you'll be meeting. Your animals are tough, look like combat animals from some of these scars. Their muscle tone's real good. Naw, tell your pal here I'm going to make these 'brids feel right at home. Give 'em a real vacation."

"Sounds good," Rockson said, taking out a gold coin from a small packet on his utility belt. "I don't know if these are worth anything," the Doomsday Warrior said, slipping it into the boy's palm so Handelman couldn't see. For all he knew the man would take it away otherwise.

"Thanks," the stableboy said in an excited whisper. "Your animals is going to shine like new, before I gets through with them."

"We must get moving," Handelman said, yawning and rubbing his large stomach which was evidently feeling empty. "There's a lot to show you. This place is huge and has enough nooks and crannies to get lost in. Why there's a legend around here about a new delegate back in '82 who had to take a leak in the middle of the night. He'd only been here a day. He left his room and apparently took a wrong turn. Never been seen again."

The Freefighters all chuckled. Even Archer, who found the idea of one's demise occurring during a search for a good piss spot to be quite amusing!

But Rock had the missing men on his mind. "Listen, Handelman, we are looking for a group of friends from Colorado. Lost them in a sandstorm."

"They might be inside, might not," the man retorted. "Only way to know is to look-see."

Chapter Eighteen

"Please, let's get a move-on," Handelman said as he led them back out of the stables, which the Freefighters were happy about doing as the smell from the place had permeated their nostrils. He led them down one of the main tunnels that led into the stadium proper. They came to another doorway, then entered a small room off to the side. Inside was a bored, bureaucratic fellow reading a book entitled, *Manual of Retrospective Recordkeeping and the Caucus Rules*.

"Handelman here, Assistant Junior Secretary Level Three. Have some weapons storage for you. Give 'em up, delegates. Rules!"

"Now wait a minute," Rock exclaimed. "I thought you said we could keep our supplies. We're not exactly the types who feel comfortable without them. I mean, where we live, every damn thing around, even flowers, are trying to do you in."

"Sorry," Handelman replied with a trace of humor on his face. "We've had too many assassination attempts—and successes—over the years here in the

Caucus Dome. We just have to put them under lock and key. Politicians can get pretty excited from time to time. And when tempers and feuds because of different points of view and what not explode—well, if you have something strapped on, you just may use it. Oh, I've seen a few shootings in my time. Including what we call the Massacre of 2067, when factions from the left and the right were voting on something that was incredibly important to both wings of the aisle—I can't even remember just what it was right now. But two or three of the Right-wing faction pulled out some firearms and opened up. Well, the left hadn't come unprepared either, and pulled out their own deathdealers. There were bullets flying everywhere. When it was over, twenty-five people were dead, chairs ripped apart, even managed to rip a hole in the plastic ceiling. Since then—no weapons. It ain't just you."

"Sounds like a fun place," Detroit muttered.

They surrendered their firepower to the bureaucrat, who took out forms and passed them out to each of them. "I'd like you to please read and then fill these out. Name, place of origin, type of weapon—you'll see, it's all there."

Rockson took an ancient, half-melted ballpoint which still barely functioned, and began laboriously filling in the thing. It could hardly be read, although the forms in triplicate beneath it still were inked enough that they picked up the information. The other Freefighters looked as unhappy about it as he did, and Archer looked positively forlorn, as he wasn't exactly the literate type.

Rock walked over a few feet to Archer, once he

160

himself was done, and began helping him with his form.

"Hey, you can't do that," the form taker suddenly said sharply. He bounded up from his crumbling, spring-popping office chair and looked harshly at the two men. "Everything is done by rules and regulations around here. Otherwise there would be total anarchy. Now, you can see, on that sign up on the wall," the bureaucrat said, as if it were the crime of the century he was witnessing, "'ONLY ACTUAL OWNERS OF WEAPONS CAN FILL OUT FORM 167B.'"

"Well, that's all well and good," the Doomsday Warrior replied with a slight smirk. "But since my oversized pal here can't write or read, in fact he can hardly speak, I'll be helping him."

Archer sort of snorted. The bureaucrat looked up at Archer, who stared back down, the right side of his mouth starting to curl up in a definite animal-growl expression. Generally, the near-mute could hold his anger. He knew how strong he was. But once in a while, when he got riled up, he started losing it.

"I think he feels bad that he's not educated," Rockson leaned over and spoke softly. "He can get pretty upset when he's mad, so—"

The bureaucrat gulped and glanced at Archer and then turned quickly away. "Well, I guess in this particular case an exception can be made," the form taker said, coughing hard, somehow pretending that it didn't really matter all that much anyway.

When all their forms were complete the bureaucrat got up, huffing and puffing from his chair, and led them down an aisle toward the back of the room.

Shelving extended for hundreds of feet, floor to ceiling. Many of the spaces were already filled with firepower. From shotguns to immense blunderbusses. The place had enough death-potential stored up in here to take on an army. One by one they handed over their own firepower, not liking it at all.

Rock gave his shotpistol but kept his mini-derringer, a two-shot affair, in his shirt. If you could hang onto the thing when it bucked, you could probably take out a wall with the mini-.357! He was going to keep his Bowie blade which was hidden beneath his jacket too, but the bureaucraft was apparently used to such shenanigans and pulled the jacket back, taking the long blade out.

"Can't fool me, fellows," he laughed for the first time. "I'm an expert when it comes to ferreting out all weapons."

Detroit undid his grenade-bandoliers and with a grim look handed them over as well. Then his 9mm Liberator went. He kept a small blade that unfolded hidden in his belt, which the form man somehow didn't see.

Chen gave his blade and a small 9mm that he carried sometimes as well. He didn't mention that he had about a half-dozen shuriken, two of them explosive. And again the bureaucrat couldn't find them when he patted the Chinese Freefighter down.

The bureaucrat reached for the huge crossbow nervously as Archer swung it back around his shoulders. He held onto the thing as if it were his first-born. And let out a little snarl again. "NOOOO BREEEAAAKKK!"

"I'd make sure that thing doesn't get damaged,"

162

Rockson warned the weapons taker. "Not even a scratch."

"Oh no," the man replied, shaking his sweat-beaded brow. He held out his arms to receive the weapon, but Archer wouldn't let go of it until Rockson gave him the go-ahead sign. Mumbling and looking quite perturbed about the whole thing, Archer then handed over his alumisynth quiver, which held all kinds of arrows. But he managed to hold onto something—his long knife inside his deerskin pants. The bureaucrat wasn't about to search him. In fact, he pulled back quickly, wanting to be as far away from Archer as possible.

And with that, the Freefighters supposedly all searched and weaponless, the bureaucrat handed each a slip of paper—the last sheet of the triplicate form.

"Now, you'll need these when you come to retrieve your things."

"Great!" Rock replied with an undercurrent of sarcasm. Though the bureaucrat in charge of firearms forms didn't even seem to notice. That was one of the good things about that type—they didn't see or hear a hell of a lot of what was going on around them, as they were usually too busy getting fat, or filling out meaningless pieces of paper!

"Okay, let's get the hell out of here," Handelman said gruffly, as he looked at his ancient wristwatch held on his wrist by a cord. "We've got a lot to do, and see." He led them down the main lobby, a good two hundred feet. They reached another wide opening and walked through.

"Jesus—" Rockson whistled through wide-open lips while Detroit and Chen just stared ahead, as if in a daze. For they were looking down over the insides of the great Caucus Stadium. Rockson had never been inside a structure so immense. It was hard to believe it was man-made, so huge was the inner main area. The huge curved ceiling seemed impossibly high. From one end of the sports complex to the other it must have been four football fields wide, perhaps two long. Steel beams crisscrossed on every side and along the plastic ceiling. Light came in from various plastic-light-sheets set into symmetrical designs. Whoever built the place had done a damn good job. For the giant sports dome had to have been completed a hundred and twenty years ago, maybe more.

Rock looked all around the dreamlike structure. There were so many levels, tiers everywhere, rising up so there were five different levels all around, circling the entire stadium. There were just a few people around, and it was obvious that they weren't regular delegates but rather cleaners. They went around in the endless rows of chairs dusting, making sure that everything would be in spotless, shipshape condition in preparation for the upcoming convention. Men were down on their hands and knees, dusting and scrubbing the floor; waxers and shiners worked on the chairs, on the walls, on the immense stage and podium that stood in the dead center of the stadium floor.

As Rock turned his head from side to side, the place just overwhelmed him more and more. From the outside of Caucus Dome, the structure had seemed huge, impossible to comprehend. But once inside, the huge structure seemed even more impossible to take in mentally. The top of the curved plastic dome, with all its beams, seemed larger than the sky itself. It just seemed to rise up and off in every direction. Rockson's eyes kept moving around as he tried to take it all in.

"Come on," Handelman said, bored with it all, since he had lived and caucused in the Caucus Dome for years. He led them down the aisle, one of a dozen or more of them. Down toward the stadium stage. Folding seats ran off in both directions. There must have been tens of thousands of seats that circled the inside of the stadium, forming tiers that circled around the entire space.

"Some son-of-a-bitching place," Detroit commented as the Freefighters followed just behind Rock, Handelman in the lead.

They walked down the aisle for a good five minutes, so much area was there to get to the center. They were all in a state of awe.

As they reached the end of the aisle, they looked across the floor. It had once been astroturfed for the games that had gone on a century before. But even the toughest material would have started breaking down after the decades. In the center of the areas of faded green covering was the wood plank platform. This was huge, too, raised up about ten feet from the floor. It was a good hundred feet in diameter. And it was centrally situated, so anyone in the stadium could see it from any of the seats. If nothing else, the whole thing had been well designed.

They stood there for a while watching the work crews tear ass all over the place. There must have been hundreds of workers moving around as if they had only minutes to complete their jobs. Rock glanced around at what he had thought were large waxing machines until he got up close. Men were driving these machines that he suddenly realized were motorized carts with

165

red, white, and blue stripes on the sides, making a loud chugging sound. The drivers wore straw hats, and had plump-faced, blank expressions. It was like America of the years just before the atomic clouds hit. The world-gestalt of a century before permeated the place, creating an aura of a time that would never exist again.

Handelman walked right up to the speaker's platform and pointed around with pride.

"There aren't a hell of a lot of places this big and still kept in such good shape. Pretty amazing, isn't it?" The man was clearly proud of the domed stadium.

Men in golf carts were scooting around the platform, putting finishing touches up with the carts' long-reaching mechanical arms. Flags were carefully set up in each corner of the podium.

In the dead center of the vast stadium, sitting on a gold-colored table approximately ten feet in diameter, about six feet high, Rock saw the strangest "sculpture" that he had ever seen. It was all rather amorphous, fused together like some mutated statue. A glowing glob of granite? No, it looked smooth, with an occasional bump, like melted plastic. "What the hell is it?" Rock asked.

"It's the Soul of Nixon," Handelman said, making a little crossing motion over his fat stomach. "Our sacred God, the Oneness! Be careful. It is not to be touched. Only the Nominee may touch it."

Rockson went closer and squinted as he tried to decipher just what the hell the damn thing was. It indeed was like a glob of semitransparent plastic, and there was a mixture of different symbols from America's past embossed on its slippery surface.

He jumped back a foot when the mass started to

glow dimly. As he watched, the object's glow grew in intensity, then various neon signs imbedded inside the thing started to light up. Advertisements! Miniatures of the kind of advertising that had once adorned the buildings on Times Square in New York City!

"DRINK KOKEY-KOLA," and "BUY JOU-JOU'S" came on; and "ROMMEL CIGARETTES—NOT A COUGH IN THE CARAVAN LOAD." But the best one was the largest—a life-size, full-color neon portrait of NIXON. "NIXON'S THE ONE. ONLY HE CAN SAVE US," flickered on and off above the smiling, waving neon picture of Nixon. And the neon representation of one of America's legendary presidents started to move. He would go from giving the "V" for victory sign to kneeling down with his hands grasping the hilt of a long golden sword that was sunk into a huge Kokey-Kola Can. The sword appeared to be real, and the end of its hilt actually stuck out of the glob of strange plastic.

Soul of Nixon my foot! Rockson thought, this is some kind of nuke-fused junk left over from the day the bombs fell, probably powered by some sort of radiation source imbedded inside.

"It's something else, isn't it?" Handelman said, almost softly, his eyes starting to fill with tears. "We found this great wonder in a nuked-out town called Reno. God in His Almighty wisdom has given it to us, gave us the Nixon-soul to worship. My ancestors brought it here a hundred years ago, when the Nominee was merely a young man. Nixon, you know, was the creator of all modern politics and debates. See that sword—no man can take it out save the Great Nominee, whom we will renominate in the ceremony

167

coming up! It is the source of power. That is the Sword of Nixon. It is our most sacred symbol of the indestructible self-nature of Caucus and endless debate." The man got a fanatical look on his plump face. He just stood there with his eyes completely unfocused, bathed in the flickering psychedelic light-display of the Nixon-glob.

Chapter Nineteen

"I'm quite a historian on the place," Handelman went on, as he focused on the Freefighters again and took off his straw hat. He waved it at some of the assembled workers on stage, and those all around the Great Dome, who waved back.

They walked around the fantastic ancient stadium, each of the Freefighters following Rockson's command, observing all, each man storing his own bit of what he felt was vital information.

"My father, bless his political judgments and forethought," Handelman said, looking up at the great dome ceiling wistfully, "was in the first vote. It is a shame he had to kick off while such a very young man. A good twenty years ago, before some of the major changes were made here, he entered the Eternal Meeting."

"Yes . . . a shame. So, how did you all survive the holocaust?" Rockson asked.

He glanced here and there at the cart vehicles, at the hundreds of workers carrying chairs, moving screens, doing various jobs that Rock couldn't even quite figure out. Everyone wore the same khaki slacks, short-sleeved white shirts, and those dumb straw hats. Rock could see, as he got used to it all, that the hats and clothing were actually slightly different from one man to another. Some hats had bands with more red, white, and blue stripes, probably a sign of rank.

"Well, as I mentioned to you," Handelman went on, turning from the no longer lit-up Nixon sculpture, "the Great Dome of the Republam Party was somehow spared the nukes. Though there was a little bit of damage on the outside walls, which was repaired quickly. Oh, it was terrible back in those days," Handelman went on with a sigh, looking up at the misty rafters all around them. The yellowish colored mist seemed to ooze down toward them from on high, in myriad, twisting streams. "Not that I was around," he went on , lifting his straw hat and combing back almost nonexistent hiar.

"We sent out hunting and exploration parties after a few months. But the men never came back. The next exploration group, as well, just disappeared. Whether it was because of radiation, wild animals—who the hell knows. But for the first years, our ancestors couldn't find a goddamned thing. A huge all-dome meeting was called. Nearly two thousand of us were gathered here when the nuke-bombs hit America. Candidates were to be picked, convention chores divided up. They decided to go on with the Convention. And, of course, the Nominee had to be sanctified. And that annual event has become our reason for existence, our philosophy: To keep the delegations, the meetings, the very

170

convention itself moving along. The Nominee is so great. . . . He helped us; no, indeed, he helps us control our lives.

"We adapted much of what we could find around here—these straw hats, the pinstripe and blue blazer outfits. And we developed a ranking system. Everything perfect in its own way. And we must be doing something right—because we've been around for over a century! We carry out the same roles that our forefathers did, the Nominee's perfect ways that cannot be questioned."

"But how do you actually survive?" Rock asked, as the rest of his team took in everything around the huge Dome, trying to pick up all the extras they could. "I mean," Rock clarified, "what do you eat?"

Handelman laughed as he swept his hand around the place. "Huge amounts of supplies, frozen and dry, are stored in a vast series of warehouses and tunnels for many sublevels below the dome. There's enough there to feed ten armies."

"But power?" Detroit broke in, suddenly realizing everything was electric-powered as light-beeping door locks were everywhere. "What about power?"

"Ah, that's the best thing of all—" Handelman went on with a sly grin. "We found that, though the original electric generators and wiring were nearly destroyed, there was a heat source below—a volcanic spring which some of our delegates were able to hook up to the power grid of the place. Instant power for over a century," Handelman said with clear pride. "Can't say that about too many post-nuke cities," the man added, pulling on his red suspenders.

171

"Nope, that's for damn sure," Rockson whistled as he thought again about slipping away from this joint.

"Anyway, we fixed the whole place up, at least my sanctified holy father and his pals did. And things have pretty much been the same ever since. This whole place is really a miracle, a holy blessing. God deposited it, and us, on this Earth so we could carry out our Nominee's divine orders."

"And those orders are what?" Rock asked curiously, over the echoing rumble of equipment working and hammers banging. Up to the plastic-curved rafters men were hanging precariously on ropes, dangling down as they made final adjustments and sewed small rips in the material of a huge American flag.

"To serve the Nominee, of course! To renominate him, over and over," Handelman went on, religious awe creeping into the sound of his voice.

"But, who is the Nominee?" Chen asked nervously, knowing from Century City anthropological classes that when it came to people's gods, you'd better be damn careful. But it also meant knowing that you'd damn better find out.

"The Nominee is the Mysterious One who comes from the great Policy Position Committee in the sky. He will deliver us all through the Election to a greater and more beautiful world. We do our thing here to please Him. He is immortal, you know. Without Him there is no order, no continuity. In fact, He cannot be explained. He is very handsome and strong. Only He can lift the Great Sword! You will get to experience the many pleasures and revelations of being one with us." Rock frowned. "Belonging is really nothing—in

172

comparison to working for Him. He gives freedom from pain, from confusion, from the Eternal Vote."

Handelman stopped and looked up. The stadium lights were slowly growing dimmer, as if God's bright eyes were growing tired. Rock suddenly noticed that Archer had not come with them along the platform.

"No!" Handelman suddenly screamed out with such sharpness that the words seemed to echo off walls hundreds of feet away. "Sacrilege! You are committing sacrilege!"

Rockson spun around and saw his friend Archer at the Nixon-glob. Archer's huge, meaty hand was reaching out to stroke the strange sculpture in the center of the speaker's platform. The mashed and melted together advertising/Nixon-promotion glob lit up suddenly. And Nixon's neon arm upthrust and gave the "V" for victory sign once more. Archer had activated something in it.

Then, all sorts of sparks began to fly from the display. Rock saw that Archer had wrapped his big hands about the sticking-out sword hilt. Nixon's neon face contorted, as if he were unhappy. His plastic glowing hand fought with Archer for possession of the sword.

The whole thing was glowing brighter and brighter, as if the statue had a sacred fire inside of it. Rockson could feel a wind rising, coming from the glob. Archer's hair stood up, charged with some primeval electricity. It was as if he had made a connection to the nuked-out old world. Energies were running wild through the thing, energies that could be picked up by all the Freefighters.

"No! Don't touch it!" Handelman exploded again, tearing his straw hat off, and starting to bite on its brim—a very strange response, thought the Freefighter leader.

"YEEESSS TOUUCCCHH!" the huge bear of a Freefighter growled. Rockson could see that the mountain man was in one of his more ornery moods. Whatever they didn't want him to do—he did.

Suddenly there were yells all around the platform and a good dozen of the carts, moving fast, zeroed in on them.

"Step back from the Sacred Nixon Soul," Handelman barked out. He made a move toward Archer, then thought better of it. Handelman was terrified of the huge mountain man, especially as Archer's face was growing redder by the second and his blubbery lips curled back like a wolf that had just spotted a wounded forest creature.

"No, Archer!" the Doomsday Warrior shouted out in his most forceful commanding voice. "Get back from the statue!"

Archer snarled a little louder, though he took his hand back from the hilt of the sword. He now looked at the assembled carts surrounding the stage with some alarm. His face squinched up, as he tried to figure out just what the hell they had in mind to do with the silly little vehicles. They hardly looked as if they could harm him. And why was everyone mad anyway? He just wanted to play with the sword.

Handelman threw his torn-apart-by-his-teeth hat at Archer. It sailed a good thirty feet, soared past Archer so he could feel the wind of the thing. Then it came back, like a boomerang, on the other side.

Rock yelled, "Duck, Archer!" He could see that the brim had been removed to reveal a razor-sharp piece of metal sewn into the hat. It was a weapon.

Suddenly the mountain man got the message and gulped hard. He made to block the hat with his arm. Not a good move. Rockson grabbed Archer by the shoulder and pulled the mountain man the hell out of the way. The hat missed by an inch.

But that wasn't the half of the commotion! The Caucus people weren't about to calm down on this case of sacrilege. Even as the two of them stepped back, the fronts of the carts opened up just below their mini-headlights. There was a whirring sound from within, and out popped the muzzles of twin 7.2mm cannons!

Rock could see now that these things sure as hell did more than carry maintenance men. Rock saw Archer start toward the nearest low-wheeled apparatus. The Doomsday Warrior knew what was about to hit the fan, and shouted again. Heeding Rock's warning, the mountain man surged across the platform, just as the carts let loose with a stream of shells that flew down the platform, missing Archer by inches at most.

Rockson did a judo foot-sweep at the giant, to knock him off his feet. Standing, he was a great target. Rock had to stop this maniac before he was full of large holes. Archer turned as he hit the floor, thinking someone had sucker-punched him, his immense arm raised to take care of biz.

But he saw Rockson lying there, groaning slightly, holding his knee, and stopped.

"ROOOCCCKSOONNN?" the giant said as he

looked around at all the stunned workers, at Handelman, at his friends. Confusion took Archer's mind off causing destruction for a few seconds. Rock patted the big fellow on the arm and Archer calmed down a little. The carts surrounded them, cannons focused on the giant.

Rock gave his best "aren't we pals" grin and spoke out to the attackers, who didn't look at all pleased. "Hey, no harm done! He gets like that sometimes," Rockson apologized to one and all. He saw Detroit and Chen ready to go at it, with or without weapons, if the cart drivers pressed on. "Just a joke," Rock said. He winked at the Caucus people. "Archer is like a kid, really. He didn't mean any harm."

"He touched the Sacred Nixon!" one of the cart drivers retorted, his finger poised right over the surface of the firing button on the cart's handlebars.

"No! He didn't actually touch it. He was just tracing the shape of the thing with his palm. Been doing that since he was just a young tree. No harm's been done. Not even Nixon's nose got a blemish." Rock could see them all relaxing if only slightly.

"All right," Handelman said, waving the carts back and tugging at Rockson's sleeve to get the damned man-monster away from the statue area.

"Why don't we get some food," Rockson said good-naturedly, somehow getting the feeling it was time to get out of here. Archer smiled.

"Yeah, I suppose," Handelman grunted back. They were in his charge, so he felt responsible for the bunch of strangers. "But please, no more trouble, okay, Mr. Rockson? Keep your fellow-Coloradoan there under control."

Rockson had seen Archer touch the sword—because of the angle he had been standing at. Archer had made contract for just an instant with the Nixon face, too. He had come in close to squeeze the huge, bulbous nose that filled the face with flickering purple and blue. But no one else had seen, evidently. Another close call.

Chapter Twenty

Handelman led them back out of the main chamber of the great Caucus Dome and down one of the many corridors that went off in every direction. The killer cart crews up on the great podium just stared after them. Then they retracted the cannon-extensions on their little war wagons. Once sure there was no more immediate danger to the Nixon-shrine, they let another slot open. Pairs of cylindrical brooms began turning slowly under the front of the carts, sweeping all the dust and whatever off the platform. It should be as clean as if the Holy Nixon were coming to walk and talk on it, this very night. That's what the crews had been told.

"Now, I'm glad to say, we're heading for food," Handelman said. He walked at the lead of the small group, Rockson right behind him. Handelman didn't want to be near the mountain man. For some reason Archer scared the living daylights out of him. How much gas did the giant need to inhale to calm down? Handelman was worried. The main thing that Handelman was supposed to do was keep things calm. If he

179

couldn't even do that, he thought, at the next general vote on promotions, he was out. They had their eye on him already, he knew that. The General Committee was watching. They had surely seen how he had let an unkempt new delegate almost touch the holy-of-holies!

The way they were spaced walking now, at least Archer was on the far side of the group from him. Handelman knew Archer was looking around at the walls and the ceilings like some gawky child. He doubted the giant would ever make a good delegate.

Rockson saw Handelman keeping his distance from Archer, his mouth holding a strange expression. And the Doomsday Warrior decided to tease Handelman. "I wouldn't ignore Archer that way," Rock spoke up. "Just relax yourself," the Doomsday Warrior went on with a grin. "He won't bother you, unless he feels your fear."

"Fear?" Handelman gulped hard, looking like a squirrel with too many nuts in its mouth. "No, no fear, everything's fine."

Archer just hummed and burped here and there as he felt the walls with his fingertips, smelled the air—all kind of neat junk lay around decaying. Ahead, faint but nonetheless clear to his nose, was the scent of food. Different kinds, cooked and fried. Vegetables and . . . meat. His gait suddenly picked up.

Chen came marching along a few yards behind Archer. If there was such a thing as "enlightenment," Chen mused to himself, then this tree-sized son-of-a-bitch was pretty close to achieving it! He just took things in stride and concentrated on what was just ahead!

Masses of delegates sat eating at a hundred tables arranged in squares, eight to a group. The place was brimming with the pale, bloated faces of bureaucrats who just dug into the steaming repast without regard for taste or content. The Freefighters were amazed at how fast they ate. "This way," Handelman grunted as he led them across to the far end of the commissary. "A miracle of mass fine cooking," Handelman said, rubbing his stomach a few times. "Just take what you want—put it on a tray."

He looked at them all rather skeptically, especially the giant. He shouldn't even be allowed to be with normal people. But then that's what Handelman's very function was in the Great Caucus Dome. Facilitation, taking firm control of new delegates—and guiding them into their proper places. So they might soon join the bliss of the Great Nominee.

The Freefighters filled up their glistening new plastic bowls, set them atop aluminum trays and walked down the commissary aisle. Rock glanced into a vast kitchen, which was steaming away with huge pots and vats. Breads were being baked, meats grilled. He noted that no one dishing out the food in the cafeteria-type line said a word. You just indicated what you wanted, took it, and headed around until an empty table could be found.

Handelman waited at the far end of the serving area, knowing it would take his charges a while. They just loaded up until there was no room on their trays. Then the new delegates from Colorado came walking down the aisle all smiles. Archer was humming or mumbling. Heads pulled back here and there at the tables when the giant passed. He was big, and smelled, and looked so pleased.

"Here, the best seats in the place," Handelman said

with a false, upbeat smile. He indicated a nearly empty long table. Three blue-jacketed eaters moved over to let the newcomers sit all together. The Freefighters threw their trays down on the table.

Rockson took a single bite of something that looked like a blue version of a T-bone steak and let a smile travel across his face. He'd have to compliment the chef for damn sure. It tasted like the finest steak he'd ever had!

"Hey, pal," Rock said, to the nearest blue-coat eater, "Ain't this food the greatest?"

The man didn't look over, just stared straight forward, as if he were dead. Rock took another fierce bite, and then repeated his remark. It was a little disconcerting to get again no response at all.

"Good food, nice around here," the Doomsday Warrior went on softly, not wanting Handelman to hear him, as the fat paper-pusher was clearly trying to listen to his every word.

"Can't complain," the eater finally replied to Rockson, noncommittally. He wore the exact same dumb-looking cheap blue suit, straw cap and red, white, and blue tie as all the other men of his rank in the Republam Party. And was about as good a conversationalist as the others, too.

Rockson suddenly noticed something. There was hardly any sound from the entire room. Oh, dishes were clanking and silver as well; steam hissed, rising from all the cooking apparatus behind the glass deli counter in the back. But the diners just weren't talking. Here and there someone said, "Please pass me the salt." Or, "Is there more water on the table?" Many of them said these words without turning their heads or lifting their eyes. They ate mechanically too. Rock counted their chews. Each man chewed each bite thirty-two times, exactly!

It gave Rockson the creeps. There wasn't anything brighter than a guinea pig on a treadmill up in any of those brain-cases! He tried another tack with the man across from him: "What's it like around here?" the Doomsday Warrior asked with a bright smile. The Republam party member sitting across from Rock actually turned and he broke into a chillingly artificial grin. It was the most artificial expression Rockson had ever seen. The lips of the Caucus man moved. His words were flat-toned. "It's-very-nice-around-here. We-work-plenty-and-get-all-the-food-we-need-here.   It-is-paradise,-praise-the-Great-Nominee." He turned back and resumed his eating, as if he had said nothing to Rockson.

"Oh, I see," Rock said, gulping some more meat. But he asked more questions. "What exactly passes for fun around here?" Rockson asked with a lewd wink, conspiratorially. The fellow eater stopped moving his jaw, turned his head and addressed Rockson like a not-quite-functioning telephone answering machine.

"We-have-much-fun," the man said with another of his dead smiles. "We-do-our-chores,-cleaning,-reading-committee-reports,-organizing. When-Sunday-arrives,-we-are-given-a-half-day-of-rest-and-I-read-reports-and-documents-about-the-next-Statewide-meeting. That's-tomorrow - evening - when - the - preliminary - speeches-and - welcoming - addresses - will - start. You're - all - very-fortunate - to - be - here - at - this - historic - occasion." There actually now was something of a real grin on the poor bastard's face. "I-like-meetings!"

"Where are you from, originally?" Rockson asked, almost in a whisper.

But just as the eater began to answer, Handelman coughed loudly, directing his voice past Rock to the Caucus man. "I think that will be quite enough," Handelman said. He stared hard at the other man, who looked down at his plate and began eating slowly, one bite, then the next. "He needs his sustenance," Handelman explained a little more softly so only Rockson could clearly hear him. "He's been working all today and through the week to get his final prep work completed for the Great Caucus Week."

Rockson nodded. But inside he was seething. It was already clear that something was wrong. These men just didn't act like real people. Oh, they spoke and walked and ate, but not a hell of a lot more.

Handelman let them all fill up as much as they wanted. They needed the special diet badly. A man is always more susceptible, more open to the great truth when he is all filled up like a garbage can bursting at the seam.

At last they all rose. Patting his large stomach and with a happy little artificial smile on his jowly face, Handelman looked around at the new men. "Well, are we all happy? Is everyone satiated?"

"Mister, if I was satiated any more," Detroit replied, "there would be some slippery floors around here." Handelman again began leading them, this time along a corridor opposite to the one they'd first traveled.

"Now, I'll give you all the grand tour—if you can take it."

Rockson's men all looked at him. They were tired. Archer particularly, after triple-portion meals, always

184

just sort of collapsed, Rock knew. All the blood seemed to drain from brain, hands, even his moose-sized feet into his stomach. But the mountain man still could walk, Rockson could see clearly. Also Archer didn't yet have that half-closed look on his brown eyes.

Rock decided to push on with the journey. He suspected that they might get into danger if they didn't learn as much as possible about the setup.

They reached the end of the long corridor and then voices blared from the dimness around the turn. Men blocked their way, men with caps that said, "Local 122, Drapery Handlers." These fellows, about two dozen of them, had a slightly different look from the others. More like worker-types, with hair disheveled, hands red from manual labor.

"Well, what have we here?" the stubble-faced fellow at the front of the gang spoke up with a dark laugh. "I didn't know they allowed 'Outsidies' in here. And look, one of the creeps is a Moosie." The others with him guffawed.

"Heeee Meeaaan MEEEE?" Archer asked, letting steam out from his nostrils.

"Ah shit," Rockson groaned. He could just imagine what was about to happen next. And he wasn't disappointed. Archer stopped in his tracks, looking down at the speaker with a strange expression in his frosty eyes. He didn't exactly look angry, more like perplexed. And it wasn't totally clear if he understood the man. But he understood his intent was to ridicule.

"MOOOOOSSE?" the giant laughed, pointing at himself. Then while the group of confronters grew silent, their faces growing a few shades paler, Archer leaned down, then grabbed around the neck the man

185

who had spoken. With the other hand around the man's belt, Archer picked him right up and held him at belly-button level. As the rest of the union crew looked on in horror, Archer swung him back as far as he could go—and then threw him right down the corridor.

He slid at a pretty good clip, sending several of his companions off their feet.

"All right, you've had your fun," Rockson said with a scolding tone. "Now, let's get out of here, Arch, before you set off a labor war."

Rock could see that the giant wanted just the opposite than to leave. His eyes were big, as if he were at his own fun-park, bowling. The Doomsday Warrior could just see the next moments unfolding. The place would soon look as if a dozen or so rogue elephants had stampeded through, tearing down walls. He grabbed Archer by the shoulder, and speaking softly but with command in his voice, led him off, past the gaggle of cursing unionists.

"Come on, you wildman," Rockson said, as he pulled him away. "There's plenty of time for that sort of fun later." Archer growled slightly, as if Rockson never let him have any fun.

Thirty feet away, the man stood up from the floor. He was completely covered with grime and grease. "I'll get you, Moose! I have influence! My men will see you at the big meeting, and take you down a peg. Bet on it!"

Chapter Twenty-One

"I hope we have no more trouble," Handelman said, coughing gruffly as he eyed Archer with nervous glances. He could hardly bring himself to look at the mountain man. Even though Rock had guaranteed him there'd be no more of that, the bureaucrat didn't believe it for a second. The bearded man was certainly a madman capable of ripping heads from bodies at any moment. He kept wishing that the spirit of the Nominee would very soon choose to bless these Colorado delegates. And make them behave.

Handelman took them into another large auditorium —not as big as the dome chamber, but big enough for tens of thousands of people nevertheless. It had a fifteen-foot ceiling, and arched doors large enough to allow passage of a herd of elephants.

"Down this way," Handelman said, pointing to a ramp going down into a lower level. The walkway was easily as wide as the doors—you could drive a truck up and down it. Rock tried to imagine what it was like here a hundred plus years ago. He'd seen films of the political conventions in the C.C. archives. There was some good footage of the delegates, who streamed in and out of these labyrinths by the thousands, the millions.

"Here we go," Handelman said. He yawned as he pushed large metal swinging doors and they flew open. "These are your sleeping quarters. It is built under the actual stadium."

There was an immense dorm-style room before Rock and his men, probably as big as the dome itself! It held perhaps as many as four or five thousand rusted, military-style beds.

It was nearly empty. Just a few men lying here and there, snoring.

Detroit whistled low. "You could house half an invasion force in this place."

Archer's eyes widened perceptibly as he looked all around in a childlike amazement. He had found and explored lots of caves when he had been out running in the wild—but nothing like this big, dark, sleepy place. Usually he didn't like being underground. But this sleep place felt big, and safe. And he was tired— not from throwing the stupid man, but from the meal.

Rockson stood and watched men push wheeled carts around, taking old sheeting off beds. They put new folded-up ones on to replace them. The beds were made up with hospital-tight corners. The floor seemed to need a cleaning, though; it was full of sticky, gumlike gunk, which adhered to his boot soles.

"BEEEEEDDDDD!" Archer groaned out in a deep joy. The near-mute walked over to one and slammed his back down on it. The legs of the bed collapsed and the whole bed dropped to the floor with a crash. For a moment or two, the near-mute got an embarrassed smile on his face. But then he crossed his arms and just kept lying on the mattress. Instantly asleep.

"That one's weak," Handelman said, making a sharp, clucking sound as if it were disgraceful that the Republam Convention should have the slightest flaw. "I'll send for a bigger bed."

"No, leave him with that," the Doomsday Warrior said. The giant seemed already in bliss. He breathed in and out deeply, and started to snore.

Handelman turned away in disgust and let a shudder run through his flesh. "Great Nixon!" he intoned, making a dollar-sign symbol like an ancient cross on his chest. "Snoring is ungodly! But, I suppose as long as he won't go wandering off breaking things, I can take the rest of you up to the show." He looked dramatically at the remaining Freefighters—Rock, Chen, and Detroit. "Okay?"

Rock nodded. They left Archer snoring. He seemed to need sleep.

"Down this ramp here," Handelman spoke up. Everywhere, Rock saw candy-striped jacketed, straw-hatted delegates. They all came marching along in unison, heading for their assigned tasks. The carts seemed the main venue of travel, and lots of the delegates hopped on one, whenever they could bum a ride.

Handelman was now huffing and puffing, even though they were heading down. He took them deeper into the labyrinthine passages of the huge structure. On the next level was a vast storehouse. It was just about the largest warehouse of junk that Rock had ever seen.

189

"Boy, will you look at all this?" Chen said as they walked along one of the steel shelving units, huge shelves that rose up fifty feet. The shelves were completely filled with junk. There were appliances of every type for the kitchen. Then a good two hundred yards of small motors, chains, and electric hammers and saws. There were sharp-toothed metal cutters, with bands as wide as wrestlers' prize belts.

"Pretty impressive, isn't it?" Handelman asked, as they all moved slowly, taking in the magnitude of the place. "And this is only one floor of the warehouse. You see, there was a tremendous amount of supplies left over after the Great War," the fat pen-scraper said. "And we've added a lot over the years—collected from travelers." His voice switched oddly, "Donated, of course."

Rockson could hear the sudden stress. What the hell was going on here? He felt enormously tired, and was having trouble concentrating. Had they been drugged? He made the "double cough" signal to tell the others that they were in extreme danger, according to mutant-instinct. His men seemed to ignore Rock.

"But this is all boring, let's move along," their guide spoke up, yawning. "Come on!" They descended another ramp, this one blackened with a huge number of vehicle tracks. They reached the next floor and looked out over a scene that was out of hell itself. Steam was rising everywhere from big turbines turning slowly. Vast amounts of steam were coming out of a number of chimney-like structures. The power plant.

Rock walked over to the nearest of the huge pistons, looked down into the deep chasms in the earth. The super-heated air only let him look down for a moment.

A red liquid was bubbling far below.

Rock pulled back, as an extra-hot cloud of steam came shooting up past his face. "And this is—"

"Our power source," Handelman boasted. "The steam from the living earth drives the electrical generators our ancestors hooked up. Heating and lighting create civilization. This wouldn't be the Super Dome, it wouldn't be anything at all but a cave, gentlemen, without this power. And we would all be savages."

The sounds seemed to grow louder from the wheels turning and gears clasping. Great doughnuts made of copper cable moved up and down around yard-thick poles that disappeared deep below. It was like walking around in the guts of some immense being, everything chugging and whirring around with an overpowering hum. And yet from the way the sounds all meshed together, everything in rhythm, the Doomsday Warrior sensed that all was working harmoniously! He felt good, felt as if all was right with the world. But something irritated his throat and lungs slightly. A strong scent that he hadn't noticed at first. Walking a few steps back to the steam geysers he smelled that it was coming from below. He made a face.

"Yes, I know it can be a strong smell, especially if you're new down here," Handelman said. "The men who make repairs here have gotten used to it, and don't complain. The smell's a mix of sulphur gas and a number of things that the earth below spits up along with the steam that we use. Unfortunately, there's no natural gas, or we wouldn't even need this whole setup. But it all works, and that's sure as hell what counts, more than a slight odor."

191

Rock pulled farther back from the steam and the thin trickle of slightly yellowish gas that seeped up with it. He again felt slightly dizzy and looked over at Detroit and Chen, who both nodded slightly in the affirmative as if they felt it too. Handelman began leading them off again.

Rockson noticed large plastic pipes that a man could crawl through, about two dozen of them placed all around the generator room. They came up out of the sides of the spinning generators and led off into the walls around the place. Huge blowers, much quieter than the rest of the machinery, blew the yellowish, smelly gas off into a huge duct system, which disappeared into the ceiling above.

"Is that a venting system?" Rockson asked Handelman, who nodded nervously and wouldn't look Rock in the eye.

"Yes," he replied, in a rote manner, softly. "If we let all the gases build up in there, the sheer pressure would explode the whole stadium."

They were led up more corridors, passed more huge doors and at last came to a small, wood-paneled auditorium built off on the side. Maybe a hundred by twenty-five feet. It was a movie theater, with a movie screen and plush velvet-covered seats.

Rockson had never actually been in a movie theater like this but he knew, from readings of America's past, that they existed all over the place, though he doubted back then the seating was quite as plush as here. The Freefighters sat and leaned back with sighs of comfort, as the seats were about as comfortable as they could be.

The lights began dimming and Handelman addressed them all, standing to the side.

"Now. We're just going to present a little film—it won't hurt," he laughed, waiting for a return chuckle. After a few seconds of dead silence, he went on. "The film explains our entire operation to newer delegates— everything you didn't want to know about us—except you will." He laughed again, and again was met with a wall of silence.

"Suppose we really don't want to hear 'bout it?" Detroit asked with a half-stifled yawn.

"Oh, humor me," Handelman said. "As Facilitator, I have a job to do, or I don't get paid. Anyway, it'll only take a few minutes, and then we can leave."

"Okay," Rockson agreed, "but later on we're talking about my missing men. I want to find them and get the hell out of here. We've got our own work to complete."

"Absolutely," Handelman said with that dumb grin. The lights dropped completely and the screen lit up. They saw the stadium from the air as a film narrator went on and on about the sacred duties and obligations of Republam members. About how it was such a privilege to be in a world of total order, rules and regulations. He extolled their system of doing every- thing in triplicate, extolled the lunch rooms, where a man always could find food. Raved about how it was far better than the outside world with its myriad dangers.

Rockson listened to all the meaningless crap with smiles as the camera entered the stadium. He watched blank-eyed workers performing all kinds of stupid tasks, or making speeches. Music began swelling from all around the room and the sound in the movie went up. It was like being in a sensurround Tri-D perform- ance, only much more pleasant.

The narrator had a deep, vibrant voice and the music seemed to drone louder, going through his spine. Rock smelled that strange gas that he had gotten such a whiff of back in the generating plant. As he sniffed harder he noticed the growing mist in the air. His eyes sleepily made a circuit of the room. Yes! On each side of the seats was an almost inaudible hiss of gas, which only his mutant senses could pick up.

He tried to rise, realizing they were being poisoned by the gas. But he couldn't move, not even an inch! Rock's arms and legs felt as if they were cast in concrete. The music grew more intense, swelling angel choirs were telling him how bright and wonderful life could be under the Sword of Nixon, the all-loving, all-embracing Sword of Nixon, or some crazy thing like that.

Then he was falling into a kaleidoscope of images. Everything swirled around: flags and political slogans, fat-faced delegates.

Slowly, his mind flooded with the Republam spirit, until the Dome became his world.

Chapter Twenty-Two

Rockson dimly remembered loving the movie, and then, while he mumbled appreciation for the beautiful sound track, being helped back to the dormitory.

That night Rockson had some of the strangest, and most unpleasant dreams he had ever experienced in his life. He kept tossing and turning around in his bed like a rolling pin floating around the void. Then he was in a nightmarish interrogation session with four of the Caucus people. They sat around on stools in that horror-dream looking at him with contempt. They asked him stupid and totally confusing things:

"Who are the top elected leaders of the Republam Party?" one asked—a delegate with a scar on his forehead as if he'd had a lobotomy.

"Dr. Harrod, Radall, Questel, Harris, Smythe," Rock droned out. He felt as if there was a balloon around his head when he spoke. "And of course the Great Nominee, blessed-be-His-Name!"

"What are the main rules of behavior?" a fat, jowly

delegate asked, spinning Rockson's chair to face the light.

"To adhere to the Laws of Nixon," Rock droned back.

In the dream everything was slow motion, the physical sensation almost rubbery. It was hard to describe.

"What are the laws?"

"To follow all Caucus rules. To read the rules all the time. To never be late for debate . . ."

"What are . . ."

The questions went on and on and on. Finally Rock turned over so hard in his bunk that he fell out and woke up on the floor. The pain of his fall jolted him to his senses. What an ordeal!

How did he know all the junk he had spoken in the dream? What the hell was going on? Must have been a nightmare! Clarity and fuzziness alternated in his brain. His head began to spin again.

He saw a big, bearded man rise from a collapsed bed, yawning. He wished the hell he could remember that giant's name!

Rock heard a commotion of bells. The other men were rising up all around him. Rising en masse, scratching and burping. It must be time for exercise or food. The fuzziness drifted back into his mind. He couldn't quite remember what this was all about, but what did it matter? Only being happy counted.

Bells continued to ring, and the lights went on and off all over the huge barracks. The awakened men all reached for their striped Republam jackets and straw hats.

Right. Time to get dressed, Rockson thought. He

saw that he had an outfit too. It was folded neatly at the foot of his bed. He put on his jacket and hat.

He couldn't quite remember his name. He was— Rockhead? Boulder? Something like that. . . . Close enough!

Around him he could hear the thousands of others, standing up unsteadily, trying to get the blood which had flowed down into their feet back into their minds. They mumbled things to themselves. "Do the form in triplicate." One man said slowly, as if it were extremely important, "Caucus rules allow the Speaker of the Floor to supersede the President of the Chamber on the second day of—"

The recitations went on everywhere, a veritable Tower of Babel as the awakened men recited their canons over like monks in a monastery.

Yes, there were things he was supposed to remember. What? To his right now stood men he should know. One looked Chinese. Another was black. One was an immense giant with a beard. Who were they? Now, he felt totally confused. He felt he should know who these men were. He looked into the black man's eyes. They were blank, almost dead like a zombie's. He didn't have an expression.

"Good morning, Delegate," the black man intoned with the deadest of waves. "I hope this day is productive for you."

Rockson replied with similar words as the man stood there, waiting.

Rock glanced at the Chinese, who was standing in a weird position. His body looked much steadier than everyone else's. They were all stumbling. The Chinese had the same dead eyes, although Rockson could see a spark that none of the others had. A spark that couldn't quite break through. And then the huge man gave him a huge, twisted, dumb smile. This man seemed to be enjoying life, so why shouldn't he?

He was here and he wasn't. It was a strange sensation, like being inside a balloon that could stretch out anywhere you went, but made everything fuzzy, without oxygen. He didn't remember his past at all. But it didn't matter much, either.

Suddenly Handelman came through the door and clapped his hands at him and the closest three men. The other Caucus People stumbled out all around them, heading off to their various chores. The four of them awaited instructions.

"Hey, boys, had a good night's sleep?" Handelman asked and smiled. "Well, let's move along," the man said with a quick little clap. "We've got breakfast to catch, then more films. You all will be anxious to get out into the complex and get to work. Get your hands going, really feel like a part of this whole team."

The big, bearded guy seemed to be in a totally good mood, stretching, making little cooing sounds as he put on his striped jacket—size 96—and straw hat—size 18.

"Mornin', Mr. Archer," Handelman said, tipping his hat as the rest of the men half-stumbled around dressing. Rockson glanced up when he saw a vent from which some yellow mist was emanating. He somehow realized briefly that it was a stupor-gas. That they were taking it in against their will. Alarm bells went off in his head. He should do—something.

Then the thought disappeared again, down a low screaming steel slide, until even the memory of having a thought disappeared in a mist.

"Come on, Mr. Archer, and you others, too," Handelman said with a nervous expression. The mountain man opened one suspicious eye wide, then another and focused hard on the Facilitator. But then he heard his favorite word.

"Breakfast!" Handelman coaxed. "As much as you want. If you just would be a little more relaxed about the whole event—then everything would be—"

"BREEEAAAKKKFFAAAASSSSSTTTT!" Archer yowled out enthusiastically. Handelman saw that he had at last made contact with the man. He noticed with some concern that Archer didn't seem to have a total effective response to the stupor-gas or even to the heavily drugged food. He marched them all off, the Freefighters sort of bouncing along the corridor.

None of his friends said, "Good morning," Archer realized. And they were not walking quite right. He was used to seeing Rock and Detroit, and especially Chen, who could balance on a piece of cord, walking firmly and resolutely. It was a little disconcerting to see none of that animal grace-of-motion. But his mind was not bothered by such things for more than a few seconds. He felt his heart beating fast as he approached the smells of the kitchen.

They spent about half an hour at breakfast. Then Handelman led them on to the movie. They were seated, all nice and comfy. Then Handelman pressed the button, winking at Archer. The screen lit up and they all sat through another hour of "How Wonderful the Caucus Dome Is for Everyone." A film about how choosing to live and work there was the greatest thing a man could do, how this place contained the meaning of all things—Order. It made little sense to Archer. But he had a pleasant feeling. His friends seemed to like it a lot, though. They even cheered when they saw the statue of Nixon.

They watched images of men working happily in vote-counting rooms, men making posters or leaflets. They watched men carrying huge books entitled *Rules of Voting* and *Governmental Procedure.*

"There men are all carrying out some of the myriad tasks of the Caucus Dome," the Narrator said. "They have a place. You have a place now too—with us." Archer smiled. They all smiled.

Then the images were going faster and faster.

Rock thought he smelled some extra flavoring in the air. More gas to feel good, like a baby wrapped in a blanket as Mama rocked him over and over. He liked the gas. And the movie.

After what seemed like a pleasant eternity, Rockson didn't particularly want to come out. There was a loud siren though it only lasted for a second. Rock looked up. The movie screen had rolled into the ceiling. Sitting behind where it had been was an immense, old-fashioned office chair, containing a big and ugly man.

"Welcome to our society," the old gray-haired man said, staring hard at them. Rockson felt his pleased feeling fade. He could hardly bear to look at him, as the huge decayed body was fat and pasty with a greenish tinge, like rotting bread. The seated man must have weighed more than eight hundred pounds.

But it was the tiny ears that were somehow the most striking things on his head. Oh, they were there, but sunk way back like flat gray flaps somewhere lost in his hair. He wasn't human somehow, more like a thing.

The fat man wore a long robe of striped red, white,

and blue material.

"I am the Great Nominee," the obese man grunted. "The power behind the power. The chief deliverer of rules and punishment for transgressors, as mandated by Nixon long ago. I welcome all new delegates into our world of loving sameness. Never again will there be fears, lack of food, or no bed in which to lie. You are free, like you've never been." He pushed his hands together and then let them dangle like huge blimps at the sides of his chair.

Somewhere inside, Rock felt rage, pure animal, murderous rage. He knew something awful was happening, but it was a thought far away, perception without thought.

"Say, 'Thank you, Great Nominee,'" the enormous man ordered, holding his hands to the skies.

"Thank you, Great Nominee," the Freefighters replied—all except for the mountain man, who said, "THANKSS." For athletic, powerful men, they spoke as if they were half-zombies. Their gesture of raised hands was weak. But it pleased the Nominee.

"You are fortunate to have arrived at such an auspicious time," the Nominee said, letting his hands pull back under the robe. "It is the meeting of our annual Caucus, to fill new positions, change some outmoded regulations. Handleman will assign you to your tasks."

The Nominee looked them over again as if checking out the new additions. "I'm so happy to have met you. I have pressing business to conduct, so I must leave, however. Remember, the Bureaucratic Process is the pathway to Salvation!"

"I second that," Handelman shouted. Handelman

turned to the audience. Then, like a cheerleader leading a pep rally, he shouted, "Everybody! The Bureaucratic Process is the pathway to Salvation!"

Rock and the other Freefighters joined in. "The Bureaucratic Process is the pathway to Salvation! The Bureaucratic Process is the pathway to Salvation!" While the men were working up to fever pitch, Handelman led them out of the auditorium.

They were taken to "Job Placement"—an aptitude center more than anything, tested, and then given jobs. The jobs were mindless, to say the least. Rock didn't have to be bright to put a sheet of paper in an ancient typewriter and pound out copies of a leaflet for hours.

Detroit and Chen were assigned to squeeze a lube can of oil down in the generating plant. They had to walk around each of the immense steel poles upon which the huge turbines spun, and squeeze off some oil. The turbines worked so hard and fast that they really burned the stuff up. The oil was old and not very viscous. It was a boring task, but they weren't really aware of that. They themselves worked like well-oiled machines, without a thought.

Rock was very happy typing. As the Nominee had said, they had good food and a bed. What else did a man need?

Chapter Twenty-Three

Over the next two days, as he tended to his duties, the Doomsday Warrior felt himself falling deeper and deeper into a mental and physical abyss. It was a strange feeling, for somewhere he could sense that it was all madness. But he felt like a tadpole at the bottom of a swamp covered over by ten thousand tons of mud. He wasn't going the hell anywhere.

He worked, had to work, had no other choice. The Caucus people were everywhere, supervising, running around, making sure Rockson and the other typists did their best. He didn't mind, really. There was something nice about being a typist. He knew exactly what to do, and there was a perfect place for him in this world. He had no worries, no worries at all.

It was midnight the second day on the job when Rockson took a big fall. He was coming down a set of metal stairs on one side of the dormitory, about to go to bed. Somehow, because he wasn't holding the bannister, his right foot caught on one of the steel steps and he went flying forward. He really didn't know how to stop falling.

But his body knew better than he did, having worked out, and having been attacked so many times. His body responded because he was a mutant with a few extra action-cards thrown in there for moments just like this. He managed to arch his body halfway down the stairs. There was a sharp pain in his right chest as he banged against the bannister. Rock rolled down the last fifteen or twenty stairs and cracked into the concrete floor like an artillery shell. He rolled over a few times and somehow wedged himself beneath a bed.

He could move, but only a bit. He was near-unconscious, a faint groan issuing from his parted lips. Rockson, the sleepy typist, had managed to put a couple of nice bruises on his skull. The way he was wedged, his head was against an air vent. And as he lay there, as still as a corpse, the entire group of men from his section trundled to their beds, and fell asleep, as if nothing had happened at all.

Someone eventually counted heads and noticed that Rockson was missing after a few hours. Men were sent around to see just what the hell had happened to him. But the way he had fallen, beneath a guy's bed, hid him from view.

Upstairs the work for the big meeting-to-come was accelerating. All the chairs surrounding the platform got another cleaning. Checks were made on the microphones. The speakers that would boom out the Great Nominee's sacred words were adjusted. The prep-workers stayed up all night and into the next day to make sure.

As they worked, Rockson lay with his face pressed against the venting system. After a long time, he began to regain control of his mind. It began with a headache like a sledge hammer. He opened his eyes slowly. He knew he'd been in and out of consciousness for maybe twelve hours. Everything hurt. But suddenly he knew the pain was worth it. He realized just what had been going on. He wasn't a typist in a typing pool—he was the Doomsday Warrior once again.

When he'd fallen he'd jammed his head into an oxygen vent, rather than a hypno-gas vent.

Of course. They'd have to mix in some fresh air with all that yellow gas they were feeding to the whole damned place to zonk everyone out, to control their minds.

He leaned forward and took some huge whiffs of the invisible stuff. Hmmm, it tasted good. Real good. And it cleared his mind. Shit! He'd really been careless, hadn't realized how he had been losing his mind the whole time he'd been in the dome. But now he was okay—or nearly so. Now what?

When he felt he had been sufficiently revived, Rockson crawled out from under the bed. His mind filled with a deep revulsion for the Caucus people. They were not just dull, they were a horror beyond belief. A horde of robots. The Nominee, whoever or whatever he was, kept them like mindless ants, scurrying around. Well, Rockson was out of their control now. He took another deep breath at the vent and then moved into action.

He was very unsteady on his feet and had to throw out his arms like a tightrope walker to take steps at first, to keep himself balanced. But he was okay.

First things first; he made himself plan, although it actually hurt his skull to begin analyzing things. First thing was to shut off the hypno-gas. He had to get them all off the stuff. Especially his men.

Rock walked around the vast sleeping-room and saw what he hadn't noticed at first. That there were secondary venting system openings alongside all the gas ducts. More oxygen. They fed a careful balance of stuff up through the dome. It must have taken a long time to get just the right mixture. They had built many vents. Some were devoid of air currents or gas.

It took the Doomsday Warrior a little while to figure out the whole damn duct system, but he did. He crawled down through a dead vent to the power-plant area, and slunk around, checking it out, then found the valves to cut off the gas. They hadn't been closed for a century, but with his mutant strength he managed to shut them off.

Next he opened to full every oxygen valve in the place. Before he left the area, fresh, cool air came whooshing out of every duct in sight. It headed out all over the dome.

That should clear out a few brains, Rock thought. He didn't really believe that he was going to take on this whole damn crew of this madhouse by himself, especially feeling this dizzy! He rested for about a minute, still affected by the traces of the gas continuing to float in his skull. But every second was bringing back more clarity, an understanding of exactly what had happened. Rock started getting madder than ever.

He headed out the door, managing to break the lock with a few kicks so no one would be able to get down into the valve area easily.

Many lobbies and corridors away he could hear the booming voice of someone introducing the Great

Nominee, then wild applause pouring over the loud-speakers of the stadium. It was beginning, the whole mysterious event had started. He had to hurry.

Rock headed down the corridors, searching his still-sludgy brain for information. Where were their weapons? Somewhere in this direction . . .

A guard appeared ahead, this one actually carrying a rifle on his shoulder, unusual for this lot. He raised his hands to stop Rockson. "Where are you going, mister?" the grim-set lips intoned. "All workers should be inside the stadium listening to the Great Nominee's speech."

"I know," Rock said just as slowly, as he stood there at attention. "I am new here, I became lost. Please guide me on my way."

The guard looked him over slightly suspiciously. Perhaps his eyes were looking a little funny—too clear.

There was a touch more clarity in the guard's fogged eyes too, and pain, great pain, for it hurt to be receiving pure air from the vents. Hurt to start to become conscious from the oxygen Rock had sent out all over the dome. The guard mumbled out directions for the "lost" delegate and then slumped against a wall.

Rock thanked him and headed off, making a right instead of a left turn and reached the end of the corridor. He had remembered the direction of the weapons storage area. Logic was crawling back into his brain. It felt great. Logic said he had to get the weapons and find his men. That was what he should do.

He came to a large door that read "Arriving." That was the first room to which they'd been taken. He walked in and grinned as the two guards on each side of the door did double takes.

"Hey! What the hell are you—" both men said, jumping to their feet. "No one is supposed to be in here—no one."

Rock glanced quickly around—and could see that there were weapons stacked everywhere, from handguns to huge missile-type monsters. A veritable arsenal—but too much for one man to carry. The whole crew that now filled the dome, screaming out their guts to greet the Great Nominee, had been pretty well armed when they showed up from all over.

"Oh, it's all right," Rock said, with a wave of his hand, "I'm cleared!"

They both started toward him, coming around from each side. These were big boys, presumably able to stop any would-be entrants by just standing up.

But Rockson had taken out tougher men than these two. As the one on the right reached out to grab him, Rock just flicked up with his right leg. The tip of his boot caught the guy in his groin. The man let out a scream and fell to the floor in agony.

The second one came storming in as well, and leaped up in the air right at the Doomsday Warrior. Rockson just stepped slightly to the side to avoid the drop-kick. At the same time, he pushed the man along in the air. The guard went flying forward at full speed, without the slightest chance to throw his arms up to protect himself. His face slammed into the concrete wall with a terrible crunching sound. Then he didn't move.

Rockson had to act fast and he knew it. If the others discovered the closed gas valves and stopped the oxygen from cleansing everyone's brain, the enemy would get the whole place back under control. The delegates were probably all feeling a little funny up

208

there in the auditorium already.

Rock looked quickly around at the shelves, and found the Freefighters' weapons. He felt elated to strap on his belt, and holster his death-dealing shotpistol. Then Rock took up Archer's steel bow and his quiver. He grabbed Chen's Liberator, and Detroit's bandolier filled with grenades. He knew they'd all be happy as a skunk in a tree-trunk to see their stuff. In this world you didn't want to go around without protection.

He loaded up his emptied magazine fast and made his way out of the room. The guards weren't going to be functioning for at least half an hour. His mission would either be over—or it wouldn't matter by then what they did or said about him.

He walked out and tore down the corridor, trying to balance all the weaponry and ammo in his hands and on his shoulders. Rock didn't need a map, that was damned sure. He could follow the noise. He flew up the two levels to all the screaming people. The crowd of ardent Nominee-worshippers was outdoing itself. The noise grew louder and louder until Rock stepped from a side door and saw the gathered delegates. There were balloons by the thousands—red, white, and blue— dropping from a net on the ceiling high above, and trumpets and drums were keeping the chanting, screaming hysteria going.

Suddenly, a guard started to touch his sleeve, but Rockson shot an elbow right into the man's face. He didn't know what hit him.

Rock saw the Great Nominee down on the platform. And gasped. Yes, the man from the movie wasn't human. Maybe he had been human long ago, but not now.

The Great Nominee, his huge, decayed body wriggling around beneath his overflowing robe of red, white, and blue, was standing there at the podium, holding both greenish flabby arms up, accepting the ovation. He was trying, Rock thought, to look like Moses or Jesus or something like that. No, the way he shook his jowls and waved his arms the attempted imitation was clear—he was trying to look like Nixon! Shaking those jowls, giving a crooked smile!

Finally the band stopped playing. And the Great Nominee spoke: "Perfection, that's what this campaign means! Over the past century, we of the party have achieved great things, but I say to you now, we are reaching higher, achieving more and more. There is no limit to our goals, to our accomplishments." The Great Nominee's voice bellowed out over a thousand speakers, his voice tearing around the stadium like thunder from the angry clouds. "It is through our rules and regulations," he continued, "through the order we have created to replace the hell outside, that we have created a great society. Repetition, triplication, is the answer for every problem, every question."

While the applause broke in, Rockson glanced around the audience to see how the drones were taking in the oxygen.

They weren't clapping much anymore. As a matter of fact, confusion reigned. There was a new, unsettled look in their eyes as the oxygen began to really get into their systems. And three new delegates looked very confused. His Freefighters! The Doomsday Warrior tore down the middle aisle as the Nominee went on haranguing the zombies of the Bureaucracy.

"Archer! Chen! Detroit!" Rockson screamed, as he

210

picked them out of the sixth row. He came rushing up to their chairs. "It's me, Rockson! Come on, boys, get it together!"

Guards were coming in from everywhere now as the Nominee stopped speaking for a moment. It was a pretty bizarre sight as the entire stadium grew as quiet as a desert. Everyone watched the scene unfolding. There wasn't a second to waste.

Rockson's voice and the sight of their firepower seemed to push the three Freefighters from the brainless state to total clarity.

"Rock, what the hell is going on?" Detroit said, rubbing his eyes. He actually fondled his grenades before he strapped the bandolier around his chest. Rockson smiled and held the Liberator mini-machine pistol up and slammed a mag in. He had his men. Now he was ready.

Even as the row of cannon-firing carts came tearing down the aisle right toward them, the Rock-team moved into action. As the delegates all around them were blown to little bloody pieces by the carts' fire, the revived Freefighters and their commander headed for the platform.

The loathsome Nominee regained his composure as the Freefighters came toward him, and he started directing streams of still mindless blue-jacketed Republam officials to stop them. Screaming, "Protect the Nominee!" they came at Rock and his men. The blue-jackets started tearing their hats with their teeth, to expose the razor-sharp brim-weapons. But before they could throw the hat-knives at the Freefighters, they were cut down by Rock's burst of smg fire.

"So, you wish to play games with me?" the Great

Nominee laughed, and he threw his robe off. Rockson gasped when he saw the man's naked skin.

It wasn't just that there was a pile of fat, a landfill of sludgy, greenish skin that moved around in every direction as he walked across the stage. But now Rockson saw just how the Great Nominee was able to move that diseased relic of a body so easily. All over the fleshy mess of a body were electrical wires. The man was part robot!

Bionic mechanisms around his elbows, knees, and ankles gave the Great Nominee power-boosts to his atrophied, aged muscles. The man was all geared up, super-wired, with a million computerized additions to his physique. Now, with the robe off, you could hear the hum of all that high-tech motor-equipment.

The Great Nominee turned toward the Nixon-statue which was all lit up like a neon Christmas tree. It was probable that the statue was responding somehow to the electrical and magnetic energy of the Nominee's fantastic body-systems.

What the hell was he doing? Rock wondered. But then he found out.

"Everyone look here," the Nominee shouted, "and see that I am all-powerful and that I am the sanctified one! You must all obey me!" He reached out and grasped the hilt of the Nixon sword, the most sacred of their symbols. And a hush fell over the pandemonious masses. Somehow Rockson remembered from his indoctrination-brainwashing film session that the sword was more than a sword. It was a death weapon with great destructive energy. The Great Nominee must not be allowed to lift it up, for it could shoot rays of ultimate power out. It could destroy them all!

"Stop him," Rock shouted, "or we're history! He must not get the sword."

The Nominee pulled on the shiny hilt of the sword as the Freefighters charged toward the podium. Evidently, it was no easy trick to get the sword up, so they still had a chance. But then the Republam blue-coats responded to the attempted assault on the Nominee by launching hundreds of their bladed straw hats at Rock and his men.

"Hit the deck," Rock shouted. He and his men all dove down and the hats sailed overhead and missed. Archer twisted around and managed to get one of his steel explosive arrows notched and let it go. He skewered a row of mindless fanatics who were headed his way. They fell, all stuck together in a row, impaled on the seven-foot-long arrow.

Rockson decimated a flock of protectors with a series of shots from his shotpistol. They fell, peppered with the "X" patterned explosion of the weapon's bullets.

Chen downed another three protectors with a single shuriken explosive star dart. And as the black Freefighter lobbed grenades to keep the other enemies back, the rest of the Freefighters once again raced to grab the Nominee.

"Oh, Great Agnew, why have you forsaken me," the Nominee gasped, still struggling to free the sword from the flickering Nixon-glob. He gave it one more try, veins sticking out all over his flab-body, his circuit wires shorting and sparking with the extra effort.

The Great Nominee couldn't understand it. He had lifted the sword several times in the past, and shown the delegates that he was the Chosen One in that manner.

Why wouldn't it budge now? He gave it one more try, as the enemy once again assaulted the stage.

And the sword came free. Snarling triumphantly, he began to lift it up, and turned in a swivel to direct its point at the infidels. "Oh Great One," the Nominee muttered, "destroy mine enemies, smite them down!" And with those words, the Nominee had Rockson and his men in a direct line down the blade-weapon. But when he pressed the button on the sword's hilt, nothing happened.

"NEEED HEEEELP?" Archer asked, smiling as he approached the Nominee now. The Nominee dropped the sword and started to fumble in his bejeweled girdle for a hidden pistol. But Archer grabbed his wrist. The mountain man squeezed until a green pus was oozing from that wrist, and the Nominee was down on one knee, screaming in pain.

Rockson ran to pick up the sword. Maybe, even if it didn't seem to work anymore, just holding it up would stop the masses of delegates from mobbing the stage. He found the sword was fifty times heavier than he imagined it would be, and it took all his muscle power to lift it. But he did.

And the delegates that were again attacking suddenly froze in their tracks. "He's lifted the sword. Maybe he is the True Nominee!" someone shouted.

All the delegates stopped in place and just stared at Rockson, then at the piteous sight of the fat man bending under the pressure of Archer's mighty grip. They were confused by this turn of events.

Rockson turned slowly, letting the whole assembly of disoriented delegates gaze at him holding up their sacred symbol of power and righteousness. The light from the Nixon-statue flickered and danced over the huge sword.

"No!" the Nominee shouted, breaking free of Archer's grip for a moment at least. "The Infidel is not holy! This man Rockson uses a trick to hold up the sword. He changed the gasses in the air, shifted the negative/positive electrical polarity between the magnetic field that held the great sword down! Kill him!"

The near-mute Freefighter now seized the Nominee once more, and they struggled. The Nominee's wire-circuits again sparked and flared as he struggled with the mountain man. His face turned bright red.

"What do we do?" someone shouted. "Who do we believe? Who do we follow?" The oxygen had taken hold over their gassed brains. Suddenly everything that had seemed so mercifully clear to the delegates just a few minutes before was now crumbling. Their minds felt too clear, their thoughts too logical.

It was then that a tremendous burst of power from the Nominee's imbedded servo-systems helped him throw off Archer's grip once more. The Nominee lunged for Rockson, and with a burst of superhuman strength, snatched the weighty sword from the Free-fighter's grasp. "I am the One!" the Nominee shouted. "And I say kill the infidels!"

Some of the delegates responded, others didn't. A huge mass of them began racing down the aisle, throwing their steel-tipped hats. A few of the carts came careening forward, firing their cannons. How the hell they could shoot and not expect to hit the Nominee, Rock didn't comprehend. But he saved his analysis for later, as he hit the deck.

Archer didn't dive. Instead he lunged for the

Nominee and wrestled with him for the sword.

And to Rockson's amazement, Archer managed to wrench it from him.

"Here, Archer, bring the sword here," Rockson said over the booming of cannons. "Give it to me, Archer."

Rock knew that if he held up the sword, the crowd might again stop attacking. So he ran along the stage, his .12-gauge weapon blasting down opponents, heading toward Archer.

It was then that the Nominee stopped his struggle with Archer and found that hidden derringer in his belt. He placed it right at Archer's head, just as Rockson hit him full force with a drop-kick.

The flab-man fired, but the shot went wild as he was knocked down. Then, with a superhuman flip, the massive monster got on his feet as fast as Rockson did. The Nominee leveled the gun at the Freefighter leader. And fired. But it didn't go off.

It was the break Rock needed. The Nominee was coming at him and the smirk on his face signaled to Rockson his intention. He was going to crush Rockson with a full-slam of his body. In an instant, the Nominee's mechanically assisted legs let loose with a great jump. The man spread his arms and legs like a diver doing some gargantuan belly flop down in a pool. But Rockson, using all the strength he could find, managed to grab the sword next to him, and get the Nixon-sword pointed upward. He rolled away just as the 800-pound mass of the Nominee came down on it.

The point of the Nixon Blade went right through the Nominee's chest and out the other side. A geyser of blood came shooting up, half-covering Rockson. The Nominee groaned and twisted his face around at Rock.

216

He spat out some pieces of bone and gristle and tried to say something. Then his eyes glazed over. He was dead.

Rockson sat up, his head spinning like a bloody top. He looked around. Bodies lay all over the place, some without heads, some with gaping holes in their chests or stomachs. Chen and Detroit were back to back, holding forth their smoking weapons, daring any more comers.

Archer stood on the far side of the stage. He was pulling a steel arrow as large as a harpoon out of a pair of attackers he had skewered. Once released, they fell lopsided onto the red-stained podium. And no one else charged at him. The remaining delegates were thunder-struck by the death of the Nominee.

Suddenly the nearby exit doors flew open, about a hundred feet away. Rockson moaned. Not more enemies. Not now. Please, God, no reinforcements! But it wasn't any enemy!

Rock could hardly believe his eyes and ears. A 'brid cavalry was riding in! And McCaughlin was at their head. The missing Freefighters were alive and well, and had come to the rescue—a bit late in the game. The Freefighters atop the mounts screamed and hooted as they raised their Liberator autofires and went tearing down the rows, blasting anyone who moved.

"McCaughlin! Sheransky!" Rockson screamed in sheer delight, as the remaining Caucus people looked at each other with fear and confusion, perhaps realizing that the odds had changed dramatically.

"Watch it on your right," the big Scotsman yelled out as he let loose with a stream of slugs from his Lib. The man who had been sneaking up on Rockson fell, nearly cut in half by McCaughlin's bullets. Evidently there was still fight left in some of the delegates.

As the other riders piled in behind the Scotsman, they gave their rebel yells. Their 'brids jumped over whole rows of seats. They were determined to get the handful of delegates who hadn't thrown up their arms in the age-old gesture of surrender. The riders dove from their mounts and engaged in hand to hand with the few delegates that didn't want to give up.

Rockson carefully picked off a man who was driving a killer cart down the aisle at them, preparing to fire its cannon. Archer used up his last arrow to take out a man way up on the balcony who aimed a bazooka at the stage. Detroit lobbed the last two of his grenades, taking out a whole section of seats where a group of die-hard delegates was holed up.

After that, the intense silence that fell over the auditorium indicated the battle for the Dome was over.

Chapter Twenty-Four

Rockson stared out over the assembled survivors who sat around the great stadium looking very tired. Many of the Caucus people's red and white jackets were ripped, half falling off them. Others had changed into their work clothes.

The whole place had a different smell to it now without the gasses constantly being pumped in. The Caucus people looked pretty spaced out—but their eyes had a new clarity. They were at last seeing through the lies, the illusions, the ant-like culture they had been living in for as long as they could remember.

"I am Rockson," the Doomsday Warrior said, addressing them over the huge loudspeakers. "The Great Nominee is dead. Many of your top officers are gone, too." Rockson said this all in cold, measured tones. "You're on your own now," Rock went on, repeating that just to make sure. "You were all given large amounts of a mind-altering gas over the years. You're coming out of it now, so be prepared to feel some strange things. The important thing is that you are free! You can stop worshipping that pile of melted nuclear waste you call the Nixon God."

A man in the front row jumped up. He looked lost and panicky. "We of the Caucus need your guidance, need to obey."

"That's bullshit," Rockson screamed over the P.A. so the whole audience jerked in their seats, almost having heart attacks. He continued a little more softly.

"This is an incredible place," Rock said, sweeping his eyes around the huge dome. "All of you are very lucky to have it to live in."

They looked proud.

"But you must learn to use it," Rock continued. "Those of you who decide to stay must form a new society. A free society."

They looked at one another, the concept of Freedom was so alien.

"That's right! You must do it, because me and my pals here are leaving. We don't have the time to stay here and coddle you all. We have our own city, our own people to help."

"Why don't you stay?" one of them shouted out. "Be the new leader, the new Nominee. You held the sword!"

"No more Nominees!" Rockson spat out on the floor. "You all have real votes. Vote on how to run this place. Elect your own candidates."

They all looked at one another and the place buzzed with a kind of new energy. Maybe this whole damn place could make it. But Rockson knew this place was out in the middle of nowhere, cut off from the real world. It would be hard. He wished them all luck and then gave the hand signal to the Freefighters to move out.

They rose and mounted their 'brids, having loaded them to the brim with supplies from the stadium: ammo, uncontaminated food, and water and electric supplies. They were set to go to C.C. with all the stuff their home needed.

"Thank you and good luck," Rockson said, knowing the Caucus People would have to fight and think like tigers to obtain the slightest chance to survive. He turned and headed Snorter out the door. It felt wonderful to be outside.

"How the hell did you know where to find us?" Rockson queried McCaughlin, as he rode alongside him later, as the towering dome shrank behind them.

"Oh, we managed to find some shelter—a tunnel—after we lost you in the storm," the big Scotsman replied. "Stayed there for about three days and then it was over. We didn't give the 'brids any water. I knew that after about forty-eight hours they'd get a little thirsty and head off to find some. Which led us right to the stadium. We sent a couple of guys inside, to do some scouting—and they pretty much figured out what was going on. I figured it would be nice to have a good dramatic entrance," McCaughlin went on with a laugh. "You always seem to appreciate them!" he beamed.

"Well, you did good," Rockson said. "You, too, Sheransky! I'm proud of the whole damn bunch of you, even though your techniques of attack were a little on the sloppy side. But I'm not going to talk about that now. Southward ho, Freefighters," Rockson said, turning in his saddle and addressing them. "We have succeeded in our mission."